The yellowbacks... classics of popular fiction

The yellowjackets or yellowbacks were a great series of bestselling adventure and crime thrillers that had its origins in the mid to late 19th century following on from the 'penny dreadfuls'. They virtually began the mass market revolution of the early 20th century with a clear standard format and imprint/series livery (what would today be called branding). Hodder & Stoughton published the yellowjackets in two main series with series run dates of: 1923-1939 and later 1949-1957.

As the tagline ('where thrillers really began') on the back cover implies, the imprint and series focused on thrillers that were the bestsellers of their time. This current reissue or retro revival if you will, brings back many of these masterpieces, now classics in their own way and extends it further by including key titles from that period that were either great crime or thriller or even general commercial fiction (including sub-genres of noir, horror, gothic, romance, westerns etc.) influences of their time. There are some perennial favourites and many rarities either lost or not easily available being revived in the current series. Writers and characters ranged from adventure heroes like Bulldog Drummond, Allan Quatermain, Richard Hannay or the Saint through thriller grandmasters Edgar Wallace and E. Phillips Oppenheim, crime and mystery maestros like Patricia Wentworth, GK Chesterton, Agatha Christie and the Detection club, to western and swashbucklers like Zane Grey, Max Brand, Captain Blood and even romance or general fiction classics like Hermina Black, Denise Robins, Marie Corelli or Stella Morton. These were books that had storytelling at their heart and always entertained.

The yellowbacks had both hardback (with varying design elements) and paperback (which built the series look) versions with the latter still carrying the imprint 'yellowjacket'. The current reissues pay tribute to both and use an amalgam of elements from both editions while retaining the complete yellow (or 'mustard-plaster') livery with the author's name in blue beveled type with a 'simulated emboss' effect and a white outer 'outline', and the book title in black. These reissues retain the distinctive size of the original mass market paperback and follow the three main category variations—the thrillers (crime, westerns, mystery, adventure) had blue lettering for the author's name, while Romance and softer general fiction had red; and other categories like humour had green.

For more detail and a full list of titles visit https://www.hachetteindia.com/home/yellowbacks

THE AVENGING RAY

THE AVENGING RAY

Seamark was the pen name of Austin J. Small, an English writer of thriller, detective, science fiction, adventure, romance, and western novels and short stories. Most of Small's titles appeared in Britain under the pen name Seamark, while his American publisher preferred using the name Austin J. Small. Several film plots were based on his stories.

Small was born Austin Major Small in Luton, Bedfordshire on 25 July 1894. He later changed his name to Arthur James Small. He ran away from sea as a boy and travelled the world, serving in the Royal Navy during the First World War, where he was a champion heavyweight boxer. He met and was inspired to write by Jack London, and adopted the pen name "Seamark" to comply with Admiralty regulations. He began his literary career in the early 1920s publishing new westerns and detective stories in British pulp magazines.

In 1924 he produced a western novel, *The Frozen Trail,* and three romantic novels in 1925, before publishing Master Vorst a.k.a. *The Death Maker* (1926), a science fiction novel in which a secret society based in London develops a means of destroying the human species with the help of a bacteriological weapon. He went on to write half a dozen detective novels, another science fiction novel, and many short stories.

He was found dead in Kensington, London on 15 January 1929, from suicide by gas inhalation.

THE AVENGING RAY

Seamark

HODDER AND STOUGHTON
YELLOW JACKET
hachette

The Avenging Ray
First published in 1936 by Hodder & Stoughton as a yellowjacket

1

The texts in these editions in most cases have been reprinted as is, with minimal editorial changes and by and large no bowdlerizing for political correctness; though in some editions, a few words and phrases considered archaic, or those considered offensive now, along with archaic punctuation may have been modified in places to make the text more accessible to today's readers. The narratives, language, beliefs, social mores and/or cultural depictions, in these volumes are a reflection of their times and must be viewed as such. They may also contain certain cultural, racial and gender prejudices and stereotypes that may be outdated or clearly wrong then and wrong today; but their removal would be tantamount to claiming these prejudices never existed. The Publisher does not endorse or support those depictions or stereotypes; and these books have been made available for a discerning audience that will read it for entertainment value and a chronicle/record of popular fiction of past times.

Cover design by Priya Singh adapted from the original classic yellowjacket by Hodder & Stoughton.

Cover illustration: Hodder original.

Series note: Some of the books in the series (unless otherwise credited) may have cover or inside illustrations from the original yellowbacks or early editions, and while full restoration has been attempted, some images may be grainy or faded due to the condition of the original material. The end notes or bonus material or blurb details may have been sourced from the public domain or free use publications such as Wikipedia and attribution is hereby made also allowing similar free use reproduction from here. Sources requiring further specific attribution may write in and further detailing and/or corrections shall be made in subsequent printings/editions.

Reprint specifications may be subject to change including but not limited to finishes, paper, colour sections.

ISBN: 978-93-5731-130-4

Hachette Book Publishing India Pvt. Ltd.
4th & 5th Floors, Corporate Centre,
Plot No. 94, Sector 44, Gurugram - 122 003, India

Typeset in Electra LT STD 10/12.5 pt by Manipal Technologies Limited, Manipal

Printed and bound in India by Manipal Technologies Limited, Manipal

FSC www.fsc.org
MIX
Paper from responsible sources
FSC™ C043100

CONTENTS

1

THE MYSTERY TRAIL

Gerry Windermaine, puffing gently at an ancient briar, walked as far as the bend in the little Devon lane and there, quite unconsciously, came to an abrupt halt.

It was that little bend in the lane where the wicket gate opens to the sweet glory of the garden and the stunted cedar trees raise their bent arms heavenwards as though in eternal supplication to the rain gods of all the earth.

Not that there was anything specially beautiful about the garden just then, or that there was any likelihood of the prayers of the cedars being answered that day. For breezes were beginning to sweep across the moors from the wide Atlantic far beyond; and the whole great swinging panorama of gorse and bracken, vale and foothill, was basking under a high tenting of cold blue sky.

There was a smell of fresh, damp earth in the air, with just enough tang of the salt of the Channel to give it that bouquet of hard, vigorous health that is at once the pride and birthright of Devon.

But it was none of those things that had brought Gerry Windermaine to a standstill. He had passed that way before and had seen them all many times, seen them and loved them in his own essentially masculine way.

It was a brown streak about a yard wide that crossed the lane from hedge to hedge and continued on through the bracken on the other side. Something about it struck him with a vague sense of shock, an uneasy feeling of impending horror. It was as though a rigidly level line of fire had passed that way, burning and scorching everything in its passage to a dull, minted copper, obliterating from its course every clump of heather, every blade of grass. It cut a line as true and neat as a new gravel path – a line of death, running sure as a geographical parallel across the whole face of the downs.

But there was something extraordinary, something uncanny about the whole thing. Even while he looked at it Windermaine knew that that endless line of brown had not been caused by fire. The trail along which that inexplicable Something had passed was neither charred nor blackened – nor was there the slightest trace of that unmistakable smell of burnt wood that lingers in the track of every fire. It was simply killed – withered.

On second inspection it resembled more closely the trail left by some tremendously powerful corrosive; as though an aeroplane had sped across the moor spraying a threefoot trail of virulent acid in its wake.

And Windermaine knew that that explanation also was as wide of the mark as the other. He had come down that lane a bare ten minutes before and *the brown streak had not been there*. Neither, for as long as he could remember, had the drone of an aeroplane motor been heard on the moors; Longmoor was one of the few places left in England where that new phase of civilization had not yet penetrated. No, he automatically dismissed that idea from his mind. Whatever it was that had caused that streak of lifeless annihilation, it would have to be sought in some far more subtle field than mere experimental aeronautics.

For the extraordinary thing about it was that, although the dead undergrowth still retained its natural shape and form, it literally powdered at a touch. Not only that, but the very earth itself on which it grew was completely disintegrated. Moorland earth is tough, fibrous earth. It is peaty, strong as elastic. Its fabric is stiff with interknit root-growths that go down feet deep. Yet that earth had been reduced to the semblance of finest talcum powder. It was as though the very stuff that went into its making had been pulverised back into its original molecules. It was atomized. Windermaine could bury his foot knee deep in it with no more effort than one would need to thrust a boot to the bottom of a cask of oil.

He went over and poked at the hedge where the brown streak crossed it. It shivered to dust where he touched it. He gave it a good shake and the whole yard-wide section of the hedge slowly collapsed into infinitesimal dust. It left an open gap, as square-cut as though it had been lopped out with a sickle.

Windermaine's forehead crinkled into a couple of deep, puzzled furrows.

"Dashed queer," he muttered to himself, and tried to follow out the mysterious line to its logical conclusion. But the thing seemed to have no end. It went on and on to the far horizon, never deviating an inch from the dead level line, turning neither to the right nor to the left, a dark hair-line of death, sinister and inexplicable.

That streak was not the first unsettling abnormality he had encountered during his short stay on the desolate moors. There were one or two other entirely unaccountable phenomena that had happened in the vicinity.

There was, for instance, the extraordinary case of the wild swan. Windermaine had first observed it nearly a mile away early one morning when he was out for his first ramble. It was flying strongly against a stiff dawn wind, high up, with its great wings beating smoothly and swiftly through the chill air of the morning.

And then it collapsed suddenly in mid-air. There was no report of a gun, not even the soft hiss of a discharging air-gun.

The whole area for two miles around was open downland. There was not enough cover for a dog to have hidden in, let alone a man. Windermaine himself was the only living thing on the whole sweep of the skyline. Yet silently and without any possible explanation the great bird had simply shut up its wings and crashed earthwards. It made no sound as it fell, but in the last hundred feet of its fall feathers began to flutter from it.

When he got over to it he found almost the same symptoms manifesting themselves in the bird that had appeared in the death streak. Not only the feathers themselves but the flesh and the very bones were already in a state of decay. The neck was as limp as a piece of rope; the vertebrae were powdered. And yet the neck of the swan is one of the most amazingly strong, viciously tough things in the whole of the animal kingdom. But there it was. He was staggered, and not a little bewildered.

Then there was the case of the flock of sheep over on the other side of the downs. Thirty-seven of them, and they had vanished like a puff of smoke. That's all. They had simply vanished. There was no explanation. And it had all happened between the time of the shepherd going into, and coming out of, his hut. Less than five minutes had elapsed – the old man swore he had only gone in to change a boot that had begun to leak at the sole. His dog had followed him in. Noticing it, he sent it back, and when he got out there again, probably sixty seconds after he had sent the dog out, there was neither sign nor sight of the sheep. The whole vista was barren, empty – save for the dog running round in erratic circles, whinnying with fright.

The downs had been searched for miles around. The shepherd himself, who knew every inch of the surrounding country, had quartered the ground yard by yard. The hunt was kept up for days – and nothing but a long persistent blank rewarded the efforts of the searchers.

And there was also the mystery of the flickering blue lights that he had seen rising and falling far out on the moors. That had always happened at night, long after midnight. Faint blue flickers shot up and down from a spot where there was no sign or possibility of human habitation, or any mortal agency that could have caused them. Right out there on the windswept heath there was nothing nearer that could have sheltered human beings than a long series of honeycombed caves, and they were a good mile away from the light emanations.

He had puzzled over that particular phenomenon – it was the first of them – but after a little while he dismissed it as being some curious local lightning effect, or sudden appearance of phosphorescent marsh-gas – though how marsh-gas managed to rise from the solid moorland he hadn't the least idea.

But this new curiosity, this dark line of destruction, was altogether different. It was gigantic, huge. Twenty miles of instantaneous death, snaking along over the moor without the slightest clue as to how it got there.

Windermaine scratched the back of his right ear and resolved that he would make a few quiet inquiries on his own before the day was finished.

2

THE VISION

As he turned away again he came to another halt, equally as abrupt as the first. All thoughts of streaks of death, mystery lights, mangled swans, and similar uncomfortable topics flipped out of his mind like a stone out of a catapult.

He found himself looking at a vision – in that highly disconcerting moment he could think of no other name for it – a vision of pure delight that peered at him elfishly over the wicket gate. His heart, for one breathless, magnificent moment, found itself functioning like a six-cylinder engine – missing on four at least. Almost without knowing it he pulled off his cap and stuffed his still smouldering pipe into a jacket pocket. Also he returned the elfin's gaze with compound and unconscionable interest.

In front of him – he confessed it openly and without the slightest hesitation – was the living embodiment of all the delicious feminine perfections he had ever succeeded in imagining, even in his most inspired moment.

A small, dainty little face that came down to a sweet, pointed little chin; merry, almost saucy, blue eyes that had, by some magical alchemy, captured the colour of wet wood violets and held them in shining thrall; eyebrows that were a thin, delicate pencilling of brown curving daintily above the curly lashes; cheeks as softly coloured as a Dresden shepherdess, and a mouth that was built up of a heart-stopping mixture of laughter and fun, and little red lips – the whole of it nestling contentedly under a sun-kissed coronet of rich brown hair that somehow seemed to cuddle the little head on which it lay.

That was his first, quick impression of the vision that confronted him. She leaned on the gate with her chin cupped in the backs of her hands, and Windermaine could have sworn that her eyes twinkled deliberately.

Violet eyes and rich brown hair! Cherry-red lips and a pointed chin! An association that has sent a thousand men's thoughts flying off on a ballrace of purest gold. Dark curly lashes and peach-bloom cheeks! They have led men up and up to the heights. Windermaine had never dreamed they existed – not all at once and all together. He stood very still for a single, unstable moment, and then went forward, his cap screwing round in his fingers.

"Jolly day – considering the time of the year," he said fatuously, and the revolutions of the circling cap accelerated violently. At the same moment he realized what a perfectly infantile remark he had just made, and he began to redden, ever so slightly.

He was trying valiantly to get the grapnels on his thoughts. They were rushing about in his head like a flock of lost lambs in a thunderstorm. The only thing he could make up his mind on just then was that the marvellously unbelievable had undeniably happened. He had run his head into the unique moment of his life. The utterly unforeseeable had occurred. Windermaine had come face to face with the living model of the mental picture he had been carrying under his eyelids for many exceptionally interesting years.

For Windermaine, at twenty-seven, was the despair of the maternal matchmakers. Also he had a record to which any man might deign to put his name.

At the 'Varsity he had taken his cricket "blue" as a freshman, had played for his county ever since, and was spoken of as a promising Number Three for an All England Test Match side.

He had taken his degree without recourse to icebags, and had collared the heavyweight boxing championship at the Inter-'Varsity contests two years in succession. He had annexed those laurels by virtue of a cool fighting head, a sound defence, and a terrific right-hand punch that was affectionately known throughout the college gyms as "Auntie" – on the assumption that, when all else fails, Auntie can be depended on to put the little beggar to sleep. Old Joe Thwaites, the canniest of all boxing trainers, had been heard to declare that real good championship material went on the scrap-heap when young Windermaine was born with a whole box of golden spoons sticking out of his mouth.

And when the Great Interruption sent the call to arms thundering across half the world, Windermaine slipped quietly off to Whitehall and joined up as plain Fred Smith, a blunt, unvarnished, unadulterated, able-bodied seaman. He had offered himself as a piece of the human battering-ram that went out with a song on its lips to shatter the Mole at Zeebrugge; and later, as second in command of a little grey ghost in the North Sea, he had harried the flanks of the flying monsters that went reeling back to Kiel.

But all that, as Windermaine himself would gently declare, was old stuff – old, forgotten, far-off things and battles long ago. The Windermaine who had begun walking up that Devon lane was not quite the same carefree boy who had cheerfully offered his body at the altar of Mars. He had changed a bit. He was hardened by what he had seen, tempered by what he had known. It's nice to have twenty thousand a year in your own right – but it isn't always easy. Especially if you happen to be good-looking, heir to a title – and eligible.

Windermaine had spent five panicky, hectic years in avoiding brilliant mothers anxious to offload a cargo of marriageable daughters on him. And five years of that sort of thing acts like an acid on a man of any refinement; makes him cynical, over-inclined to regard the eligible girl in the light of the Eastern mind – a piece of human merchandise brought up on a tray for inspection, to be bought, or declined without thanks, as the case may be.

A flat in Curzon Street is an excellent eyrie from which to view the passing pageant of London life. Windermaine had viewed it from that angle – and had come to the conclusion that the social whirl was not very deep, hardly worth sounding. It was all very well in its way; taken as a condiment it added piquancy to a dish – like red pepper, say. But you only want to take a very little of it – and only now and then. Nobody in their sober senses would dream of making a meal off red pepper...

Thus it was that Windermaine preferred shooting, fishing, boxing, cricket, or even a day's ratting with his little West Highland terrier – anything rather than the round of the gilded drawing-rooms with their endless relays of gushing mothers and slangy maidens. He had had so many nice, nasty, charming, uninteresting, lovely, awful, hopeful, hopeless girls trotted before his critical eye that he had long since come to regard himself as girl-proof. He didn't want them and they didn't interest him. At least, that was his firm conviction until he came to the bend in that little Devon lane.

The next thing he knew was that he was standing in front of her, twiddling his cap like an overgrown schoolboy and making a perfect ass of himself in half-a-dozen distinct and separate ways. Furthermore, he was aware of it, and, what is infinitely more, he didn't care a hoot. Some fellows are like that; their hearts are so much on their sleeve that a blind Cupid could hit it.

The vision smiled delightfully and spoke.

"Gosh!" thought Windermaine, "that's not a voice – it's a trickle of music, played on silver bells."

Candidly, it was no such thing. It was just a charming feminine voice, soft, low, and musical. But it emphasized Windermaine's complete disruption.

What the vision said was, "Goodafternoon to you. My very contrite apologies, but I'm afraid I didn't quite catch what you said."

"I'm very relieved to hear it," said Windermaine. "And, anyhow, it *is* a jolly afternoon – ten thousand times jollier than it was sixty seconds ago."

"That's very nicely said," replied the vision, demurely, "but tell me, where's Mack?"

Windermaine looked at her in surprise.

"Mack? I didn't know you knew Mack," he said. "How did you know I had a dog?

The vision laughed again. "Oh, Mack and I are old chums," she said. "I've seen him with you often when you've been out together, rummaging along the hedgerows and over the moors. He comes over sometimes and cadges bones in a most shameless manner."

"It's very odd that I should never have seen you before. Have you been staying here long?"

"For years and years. I live here."

"Remarkable. I used to pride myself on a fairly observant eye, too. But I swear I've never caught so much as a glimpse of you. Do you go into hiding when you see a man coming over the hills?"

"Hardly that."

"Oh, well! I'm sorry I don't live here, too. I'm only here for a few days."

"Yes, I know. You're staying at Deepvale Manor, aren't you?"

"Yes. How did you know?"

"Well, the locality is not quite so thickly populated that one doesn't hear of new arrivals. And anything fresh happening at the Manor House is regarded as tantamount to public property. With the exception of the daily newspaper there's nothing much else to talk about or discuss, is there?"

"I suppose there isn't. Pretty empty sort of a hole altogether, isn't it?"

The vision inclined her head in definite agreement. "But that being so, what made you come down here?" she asked.

"Oh, I don't know. Sir Robert Harrigan, over at the Manor, offered to be my host for a few days – asked me to come down and chase rabbits and keep him company for a bit; and – and having nothing better on hand I suppose I just packed up and came down." Under his breath he added a fervent "Thank Heaven!"

"Weren't you over keen to come?"

"Yes and no. Harrigan is a blunt, outspoken, John Bullish sort of an old boy, as you probably know, but the wording of his letter was so – er – how can I put it? – so vaguely full of hints and hidden meanings – that I was rather interested." His eyes moved for just the tiniest fraction of a second to the trail of the dark line of death.

"Then, really, you don't intend staying very long?" she inquired, innocently.

"I hadn't intended to – but" – he looked at her squarely – "all things considered, I think I shall be staying on now until—"

"Yes?"

"Until I've grown tired of being a neighbour of yours. I suppose that *is* your little cottage over there at the back of the rose garden?"

"Well, yes, I stay there occasionally."

"Not always?"

She laughed again and shook a finger at him. "Now you're beginning to ask questions which no self-respecting rabbit-chaser would dream of asking," she said. "I'm afraid you need something to occupy your mind. Why not take that pipe out of your pocket – and for goodness' sake smoke it? You'll be burning something in a minute and blaming me."

It was Windermaine's turn to laugh. But he took her advice. In a minute he was sitting on the side support of the little wicket and she was leaning against the gate outside it.

He noticed that she had the daintiest little feet he had ever seen. He vowed she could have got into Cinderella's shoes without the slightest need of a shoe-horn. Also that she was wearing the prettiest little print dress ever made. It seemed to have come straight out of granny's laundry basket; the faint fragrance of old lavender was still upon it.

"I say," he said frankly, after a pause, "it's difficult to keep up a conversation like this. Won't you tell me your name?"

"Difficult? But why?"

"And silly, too. It's perfectly delightful finding oneself living within a mile of" – he reddened as he said it – "so bewitching a neighbour as you; but all the bloom goes off it if one can't stop and have a little chat on meeting. Don't you think so?"

"Ye – es; perhaps so."

"Well, my name is Geoffrey Windermaine, middle name Fitzalan. Dashed silly bunch of names to give a chap, but there you are. Parents are like that. Seem to take a delight in inflicting old family patronymics on poor little blighters who can't defend themselves, they being mostly of an age when their fighting weight, trained down to an ounce, is about ten pounds nothing, flannel and bib thrown in. But there it is – that's the whole devastating confession – Geoffrey Fitzalan Windermaine: known as Gerry for short, and safety. Won't you tell me yours?"

"Well, if you feel you *must* stop and talk to strange young women in country lanes, suppose you call me Rosaine?"

"Delightful – in everyway. But – Rosaine what?"

Windermaine almost thought he saw a quick, frightened look slip in and out of her eyes at that question. For the life of him he couldn't be sure, but to his own discerning eye it looked suspiciously like it. The thing was all wrong, and utterly absurd, of course, but there it was. Her answer, moreover, in some odd way justified it.

"Rosaine," she said quietly. "Just plain Rosaine. Nothing more than that – if you please." The colour had gone mounting up to her cheeks in rising waves.

"Good heavens!" thought Windermaine. "Now I've put my foot right in it. Clumsy lout! Always doing the wrong thing where the ladies are concerned."

But aloud he muttered, "So sorry. Didn't realise I was treading on thin ice. Rosaine, then, let it be. I shall—"

"Oh, please don't apologise" – there was a note of unhappiness, almost of bitterness, in her voice – "you can find out all about me from your host. Sir Robert Harrigan won't mince matters, believe me. Neither, for that matter, will his daughter. Quite a nice girl, Valerie Harrigan – she returns tomorrow from her finishing school on the Continent, but she is as impressionable as her father. I hope you like her – Gerry. It will be uncomfortable – and difficult for you if you don't, won't it?"

Windermaine was staring at her, screwing round on the gate-post so that he could face her squarely. After a long while he got his thoughts into words. "Neither difficult – nor uncomfortable," he said, with quiet decision. "So far as I know I've never met the lady, but, believe me, the presence of Valerie Harrigan won't matter any more in my young life than a row of beans. What makes you mention her?"

"Women, my dear Mr Windermaine, are always uncharitable to their own sex. And I'm afraid Miss Harrigan is no exception. Look around you, all the way round that far horizon, miles and miles of open moorland – and there are not more than thirty human beings in the whole wide sweep of it. But such of us as do exist here know one another's lives backwards and inside out; our histories are common knowledge, our doings are common gossip. We are known and respected – and understood. All—" she broke off and turned her head.

"All save you, eh, little Rosaine?"

The vision nodded. She was no longer a little imp of smiling mischief, but a pathetic soul very near to tears.

"Yes – all save me," she said tremulously. "You see, I'm the newcomer, the alien. I was not born of the soil here. I did not pitch my tent in these old Devon hills till I was eighteen. Old enough to start tongues wagging and—"

She turned away and looked up the lane.

"Here comes Mack," she said, with a forced effort. "Looks as though he's pleased with himself, too. Had good hunting, perhaps. I think you had better accompany him home, Mr Windermaine. You may not be so pleased to see me tomorrow. I think I'll be going in. It's getting chilly."

Windermaine slid off the gate-post.

"About tomorrow," he said, firmly. "Suppose we make a definite time. Say four o'clock, here by the wicket gate." He put his hand very gently on hers. "I shall be here, Rosaine; and – and I shall be disappointed if *you* are not."

The vision did her best to smile again, but it was an uncertain effort. As she walked away up the old garden path Windermaine called softly from the wicket gate, "By the way, Rosaine, what is the name of this little lane? I'd hate to forget it now that I've found it."

Rosaine turned her head for just the barest moment and her eyes, bluer and deeper than ever, looked full into his.

"Heartsmeet!" she said, quietly, and turned and walked on.

Windermaine watched her till she was lost to sight. Then, with his heart full and surging over with the queerest mixture of emotions he had ever encountered, he swung away down the lane to the winding track that passed for a road in that wild spot.

He had reached the end of Heartsmeet and was turning into the footway when, far out over the moor, he saw the figure of a tall, immensely powerful-looking man striding along through the undergrowth. There was a queer huddled appearance about him, caused by a continual attitude of stooping over at the shoulders. He marched along in sombre silence, a gloomy, sinister figure in a wide-brimmed black felt hat and a long black ulster cape that hung low over his great shoulders and gave him the appearance of a human bat of evil omen. On and on he went with his head thrust forward and his hands motionless at his sides in the pockets of the flapping cape.

Windermaine watched him in grim silence. It wasn't the first time he had seen that shambling figure prowling about over the moors. He had seen him in the mists of the early dawn, stalking along like a black, silent shadow through the gorse and the dew-wet hedges; he had seen him by the light of the moon when the hoot-owls were calling and the cry of the lone peewit sounded like the scream of a lost soul ranging the empty shore.

The figure did not pause till he came to the tenuous line of the brown, withered streak. Then he stopped and went down on his knees, fingering the pulverised earth and examining it minutely. When he got to his feet again he walked straight back up the line to the clump of cedars. Without pausing he went through the gap in the hedge, up through the little path in the garden, and let himself into Rosaine's cottage with a key.

Windermaine, with a brow as black as a thundercloud, walked on to Deepvale Manor.

3

"WILL YOU MARRY VALERIE?"

Eight o'clock chimed melodiously from the great clock on the mantelpiece in the dining-room at Deepvale Manor. The butler had just placed coffee and a decanter of liqueur brandy on the snowy tablecloth. Windermaine lit a cigar and watched the old chap glide noiselessly out of the room.

It was a magnificent apartment, panelled in oak that was black with age, carved by old masters of a long-forgotten past. Between the panels hung priceless pieces of Gobelins tapestry, under glass. The lamps were covered with deep ruby shades that reflected the light in flash-prints of crimson fire from the glittering table silver. The sideboard at the far end wall was twenty feet long, with a history that went back as many generations.

Everything in every room in Deepvale Manor bore the same unmistakable stamp of age and perfect taste. For Deepvale Manor was almost as old as the ancient hills that hemmed it round. Its history went back into the misty past of Devon's mighty tale. It was old, old and respected, long before the first smuggler landed his lace and brandy and tobacco on the wide, lonely beach in the blackness before the dawn, or the first wrecker placed his light on the Judas headland above the bay. Deepvale Manor had seen all that, and stood its quiet, unwinking vigil over it all, growing richer and richer as the years passed, and finally endowing the line of the Harrigans with a heritage that would last till eternity.

Windermaine pushed his chair back as the door closed behind the butler's back. He blew a whiff of smoke at the lamp and faced his host fair and square.

There was a little silence that became positively electric: an atmosphere of strain was creeping into the very air.

Sir Robert eyed his guest almost diffidently for a moment, and then made a forced effort to come to grips with himself.

"Are you – are you enjoying your stay here, my boy?" he asked.

Windermaine allowed the question to float past his head.

"Exactly why did you invite me to Deepvale Manor?" he demanded, firing his challenge like a rifle-bullet on the bull.

Sir Robert did not reply for some little time. He fingered the flashing diamond in the centre of his white dress-shirt and studied the glowing end of his cigar.

"I've been waiting for that question for nearly a week," he said at last.

"That's no answer, sir. Why?"

"Well, it's an interesting country round here," muttered the baronet, awkwardly. "Bracing – healthy, strong winds and the open sea – and—"

"Bosh! You didn't ask me down to admire the local scenery. Interesting country? There's miles of it all round England? Bracing? The East Coast beats it hollow. Healthy? I'm as full of health as a young buffalo. Strong winds? I can get yards of that stuff even in Piccadilly!"

Harrigan cleared his throat. He looked at the younger man from under white, handsome brows. He was a striking-looking man, a fine-looking man, with white hair and strong, fearless features. His was a face that had reliability, faith, and loyalty written all over it. The clothes he wore became him as perfectly as a golden crown becomes a royal head.

He was fitted with an atmosphere of peace and eternal quietness, housed in a manor that a duke might envy; he seemed to belong to the great, wide, restful, sweep of the moors, to be part of the very nature of it; a man who deeply and sincerely loved the wild loneliness in which he lived.

And yet, at the back of his manner, there was some half-felt feeling of anxiety, as though a vague apprehension, continually hanging over him, was being pushed deliberately out of his thoughts – and leaving its mark on him.

To Windermaine there was something incongruous about it. The whole thing was contradictory, a direct inversion of all that was reasonable and natural. Harrigan was a man who looked as though fear was an emotion that had no part in his nature, a man who was an utter stranger to nervousness. And yet, just then, he looked to be a man who was literally rubbing shoulders with fear.

"I still want to know why you asked me to stay down here with you," said Windermaine, quietly.

Harrigan returned his gaze.

"For two reasons, Geoffrey," he said.

"Well, that's a beginning, anyway. What's the first?"

"If you haven't already discovered it for yourself, boy, you may as well never have left Curzon Street. I must have overrated your powers of observation as well as your intelligence."

The note of misgiving was present in the baronet's voice; it was alive in it, the tone of a man who is wrestling with a mystery that has got entirely beyond his powers to understand or elucidate.

"I was hoping you would have noticed things down here – things one can't very well describe – the kind of things that make a man wonder whether he is sane, or whether he is going stark, staring mad and hypnotising himself into playing bedfellows with hallucinations. I'm sorry. I shouldn't have worried you. Probably the loneliness down here has got into my brain and I am seeing things that – that have no foundation in fact. I must get away – get away to Paris or somewhere where there's life, gaiety, laughter – a tonic for nerves that have all gone wrong."

"But supposing I *have* seen things down here—"

Harrigan looked up quickly and drew in a long breath.

"So – you have, have you?" he said slowly.

Windermaine inclined his head ever so slightly.

"Yes," he said quietly. "I've seen one or two things out there on the moors that have made *me* rub my eyes and wonder whether I was dreaming or not. Pretty incredible things – things that sort of make you gasp and wonder what's brewing out there under the moon. If you've seen this same kind of thing that I've seen during this last few days, you needn't worry about your brain nor your nerves – they're all right. You're not going crazy. It's all too real."

Harrigan was silent for a while. He seemed to be pondering his next utterance, trying to force his thoughts down to the believable.

"What do you make of it, sir?" asked Windermaine suddenly.

"My boy," said the baronet, "there's something going on down here that makes a man's heart quail when he comes into contact with it. I'm not frightened – don't think that, please. But – when things begin to rub shoulders with the inexplicable, when one sees things every day for which there is no possible explanation – things that begin to assume nightmarish proportions – I feel the need of youth, the strength of youth, around me.

"Geoffrey, this business has got to be probed to the bottom. To the very bottom. We shall be tampering with forces beyond our wildest imaginings, but – I've seen things happen out there on the moors that have turned my white hairs whiter, things that have made the hours of darkness a horror. That beautiful daughter of the Devil in Rose Cottage knows more about it than is right for any human being to know. She's blanketed in mystery, ringed round with it. There's something dreadful about the whole place. But I'll find out the truth about it if I have to strangle her with these two naked hands.

"Tell me, boy" – the older man leaned earnestly across the table – "tell me that you will stay down here till we've threshed the matter out, every single stick and stone of it."

Windermaine looked at him sitting there, anxious, restless, frightened of something that seemed to hold hands with the unknown. In his eyes – and all in that moment – there had come a look of icy hostility, and the poise of his head had taken on a wintry, aggressive angle.

Coldly and deliberately he changed the conversation. Harrigan had no inkling of the wicked knife that his words had sent like a white-hot arrow through the younger man's soul. He was looking only for an answer, waiting only for Windermaine's assurance that he would stay on in Deepvale Manor and help with his brains and his courage to unravel the horrors that brooded over the downs.

"You said you had two reasons for asking me down," he said, flicking the ash off his cigar. "You may take it that the first is satisfactorily understood and accepted. What is the second?"

The baronet's face cleared. That was answer and question all in one. He knew he could count on his friend. He looked as though a giant load had slid off his shoulders. His face almost lit up with pleasure and he smiled his relief.

"Ah – the second, Geoffrey, is even more – more intimate than the first," he said.

"Well?"

"My daughter Valerie returns tomorrow from Italy. A nice girl, Geoffrey. And you have been single too long."

Windermaine looked at him hard.

"I don't quite get the drift," he said, distinctly.

The baronet smiled again. "You will in time, boy," he said. "Why not consider it? There are not many like Valerie in these modern days of feminine intolerance. She's young and a sweet-natured girl. She has not been spoiled."

"And that," said Windermaine stiffly, "was really why you asked me down?"

"Yes," said Harrigan, gravely, "I want you to marry Valerie."

4

THE MAD SCIENTIST

Windermaine blew a series of smoke-rings at the ruby lamp. Harrigan watched him, dimly conscious of having offended the canons of delicacy as laid down by the particular observances of his guest. There was something in Windermaine's manner that told him he had trespassed on very private ground. He was perturbed and not a little surprised. He had thought that the young man was not unfavourably impressed where Valerie was concerned.

"You are not annoyed, boy?" asked the baronet gently, from his side of the table.

"Not even faintly amused," said Windermaine.

"I – I thought – or I had hoped – you might have read between the lines of my invitation to you." Harrigan was almost apologetic.

"I didn't. I only came down here to get away from this sort of thing. I thought matchmaking was peculiarly the preserve of the more elderly elements of the opposite sex. I never dreamed of having to contend with it from you, Sir Robert."

Harrigan looked away uncomfortably. He had been looking forward to the wedding of Gerry and Valerie so long that he had almost come to regard it as something that was understood and arranged for by Fate years ago.

"You timed my visit to coincide with her return from Italy?" Windermaine put the question as though he had been thinking the whole thing over and proposed coming to a definite understanding on the matter once and for all.

Harrigan nodded gravely. "Yes, I had hoped it would have been a pleasant thought for you."

Windermaine looked up sharply. "Pleasant?" he said, with a touch of asperity. "There is certainly nothing *un*pleasant about it. Valerie is a charming girl. Please don't try to ascribe to me opinions I have not the faintest intention of expressing. That's not cricket."

Harrigan looked mollified. "Two years since you last saw her," he said. "A long time, Geoffrey. And she thinks a lot of you."

"Oh? And why should you think that?"

The baronet smiled. "Who but a father should understand his own daughter? Valerie is really very fond of you. It's a little difficult, talking like this, after – after the way you received the idea."

"Bit of a shock, that's all – coming from you. I don't seem to be able to raise a thrill over this sort of thing. Doesn't seem to fit in with my ideas of sentiment or the sweeter conception of marriage. There's something cold-blooded about the whole presumption of a wedding by arrangement."

"Suppose we leave it at that, my boy? Leave the future to look after itself. I'm sorry if I butted in where even angels shouldn't tread. But, as you know, I'd like to see you looking after my little girl before I die. It's a matter that is very near to my heart. I'd dearly like to see it come about. Perhaps it may – even sooner than you expect, I think a week with Valerie will provide its own happy answer."

"Well, it looks like being a fine day tomorrow," said Windermaine deliberately. The baronet smiled.

"Have a good run today?" he asked.

"Very," said Windermaine. He said it so decisively that Harrigan looked at him oddly.

"Rabbits?"

"Not a sign of one. Much finer hunting than that."

"Oh – in what way?"

Windermaine smiled. "Tell me – who is that girl in Rose Cottage?" he asked.

Harrigan heaved round in his chair. "That *who?*" he demanded.

"So sorry. That daughter of the Devil, I think you called her."

Harrigan's face was so intense that his brows almost obscured his eyes. "Where did you meet her?" he asked.

"Delightful little place called Heartsmeet," said Windermaine, blandly. "Wouldn't have missed it for all the gold in the Rand – or all the rabbits in Devon. How long has she been here?"

"Not long. And the sooner she goes the sweeter the neighbourhood will be. She's a bad lot, Geoffrey. And there's something worse in her than merely being a bad lot. There's something malign about that girl. I'm ready to swear that she knows more about the frightening things that have been happening down here than anyone else on the moors. Everything that you and I have seen, the grim things, the portentous things that slide themselves under our eyes, have all happened within a mile of Rose Cottage. The other day I saw a hare belting up that lane as though half the Devon packs were on its heels. On it whizzed, like a furry brown comet – till it got abreast of Rose Cottage. And there it collapsed. Turned about ten complete somersaults and then dropped over on its back.

"I went over to it, amazed. There was no sound, no crack of a gun, no hiss of a bullet, no nothing – just a strong, virile little animal killed in mid-career. It felt and smelt as though it had been dead for a week. Ghastly, uncanny. I was walking away when I heard footsteps coming up through the rose trees in that garden. I hid myself. That girl came out of the gate, picked up the dead hare on a tray, and took it in. Now, how do you account for that? She couldn't have seen that hare go over from the windows of Rose Cottage. The whole place is hidden. She couldn't even see me."

"Very odd," said Windermaine quietly. "Very odd indeed. But you surely aren't condemning her for a sorceress on the evidence of a single incident – and one that may have a purely coincidental explanation?"

"No, I'm not!" retorted Harrigan with some heat. "But I've not lived in this neighbourhood all my life without getting to know the character of its inhabitants pretty thoroughly. I'm a little tin god in Deepvale – lord of the manor and justice of the peace. Things happen here with my consent and approval. I'm sort of temporal godfather to the lot of them. And I know them – all of them except the mysterious devil in Rose Cottage. Nobody here has a good word to say for her. She's shunned. And the people hereabouts are kindly, neighbourly folk. They—"

"Ever spoken to her?" inquired Windermaine, breaking in on him.

"No – and I hope I never shall."

"Not exactly noble to brand a girl unheard, is it? Even a dog cannot be shot as a public nuisance until its case has been heard by a magistrate. Rather cheap, I think."

"Geoffrey, she's a bad influence, I tell you – and in more ways than that. The girl is living with a man!"

"Is she, indeed? Who?"

"A slinking and sinister brute called Carlo Damian. A creature of the night. You only see him when he's about half a mile away – a gaunt, gigantic figure in black, stalking over the moors like a shadow of Death over a sunny landscape. A malignant brute. You'll find, my boy, that Carlo Damian is the moving spirit at the bottom of all this devilry that's going on. 'The Mad Scientist' – that's what they call him down here. There's never anything ghastly or inexplicable happens anywhere on these moors but what Carlo Damian has been observed in the immediate vicinity. And she's with him. All the neighbourhood knows it. Is it reasonable to suppose that a whole community of friendly country folk would shun a single one out of their number, avoid her like the plague, unless there was some very adequate cause."

"How many of them round about here have ever spoken to her?"

"How do I know? Probably none of them."

"Quite. That's the way of the world. And of country parishes particularly. Give a dog a bad name and hang it. Who gave that girl a bad name? You don't know. I don't know. It just happened that way. She's got it. You've done your bit towards it. It's the same old tale of country bigotry, the petty jealousies and poison-tongues of little communities. She's a stranger within your gates – she cannot be anything more than a thorough bad lot! How do *you* know she's living with Carlo Damian?"

"Common knowledge in the village, my boy. He's been seen in Rose Cottage scores of times. To my definite knowledge he has been actually living there for several years. Not all the time, mind you – and that only makes the matter more heinous – for he is one of those queer creatures who are apt to vanish mysteriously for months at a stretch. Nothing is seen or heard of him, his looming shadow is not seen on the moors, things begin to quieten down and horrors cease to happen. And then one day – or one night, rather – he is seen again, a slinking figure under the glitter of the stars – and the horrors begin again."

"Always near Rose Cottage?"

"Always. Things may have happened farther afield. But if so I've no knowledge of them."

"Well, if that is all the definite evidence you have against the little tenant of Rose Cottage I should try to cultivate a more charitable regard for my fellow-creatures if I were you, Sir Robert."

Harrigan frowned again as through a new line of thought had suddenly occurred to him. "You seem to be taking an extraordinary interest in this most undesirable person?" he said, agressively.

"Well, sir, am I required to offer my interests to you for censorship?"

The older man pulled himself up short and a slight flush spread across his face. "I'm sorry, boy – forgetting myself in the heat of argument."

"Cheers! Good health," said Windermaine, and raised his glass.

Then, in rather chastened tone, the baronet pleaded with him to have as little to do with the siren of Rose Cottage as he possibly could.

"But why don't you turn her out of her cottage? You're her landlord. The place belongs to you."

"She has a lease of it – or, rather, Carlo Damian has. He's the tenant. The girl came along as an afterthought. I would if I could, and be glad to – Hallo, what's the matter with the lights!" His voice rose to a half shout and there was a note of sudden alarm in it.

The red-shaded lights had begun to act in an unaccountable manner. Very slowly they began to fail, losing power as gradually and as steadily as though the illuminant was gas that was slowly being turned off at the main. Through the great leaded windows part of the east wing of the house could be seen; lights were visible in several of the rooms and they were all acting in the same way.

"Power giving out at the station," suggested Windermaine, stolidly.

As though to give him the lie the lights immediately leapt into brighter brilliance and began to glow with a strange and added glitter that was much stronger than the normal strength of the bulbs.

"Main fuse going – all the lights will go out in a jiff," declared Windermaine.

But the main fuse appeared to be holding the strain. For a few seconds the light grew stronger and then began to assume an unearthly violet tint. It glowed with the curious effect of ultra-violet rays, and Windermaine began to feel his skin pricking. Not from fear or alarm, but purely as a direct result of the mysterious rays emanating from the lamps.

"That's queer!" he muttered, and looked at his hands. They seemed hot and dry – like skin that had been too severely treated with potash. There was a harshness about them and the nails looked blood red.

He looked up at Harrigan. His host had risen to his feet and was standing under the group of lamps, staring up at them, trying to elucidate the cause of the phenomenon. Subconsciously he began to rub the backs of his hands. His face seemed drawn in putty – dead, lifeless – and there was an eerie shade of hectic colour in it, like that of a man with a heart attack on a bitingly cold morning. Windermaine, too, found himself rubbing his hands – and the rubbing hurt. His skin had become extraordinarily tender. The merest rub of the harder skin of the palm of his hand seemed to sear it as though with an uncomfortably hot iron; and there was a prickling sensation as though each time his hands met they made contact with a slight electric current. The air itself seemed loaded, oppressive.

"Heavens! What's happening to my hands?"

Harrigan, holding his hands out incredulously before his astounded eyes, was looking across at Windermaine with something very like consternation. His hands were covered in blood. His thoughtless rubbing, while all his attention was focused on the streaming lights, had actually broken the skin. It was almost as though the first skin had been rubbed away in places and the secondary skins, having lost all virility and support, had broken down at a mere touch. Drops of blood fell from his finger-tips.

"Geoffrey! What is the matter? My hands are burning! I'm maddeningly hot. And your face is horribly discoloured."

Out in the great hall they could hear the frightened voices of the servants, striving to keep their agitation within the limits of hoarse, breathless whispers, but only achieving greater penetration because of it. And they were making no pretence at hiding their fear. Something was happening in Deepvale Manor that was beyond their bounds of comprehension. They couldn't even begin to understand it. Their inability to explain away the inexplicable evinced itself in the first dangerous glimpses of panic.

They heard the great front door pulled open and some of the girls rush out, frightened out of their lives, seeking only to get out of range of the stinging rays.

Then a calm, orderly voice broke in upon them – the voice of Hawkins, the butler.

"Now, ladies; no hysterics, please. Not in Deepvale Manor. Come in immediately. If you will control yourselves for a few moments I will go and inquire instructions of Sir Robert."

There came a single abrupt knock on the door and Hawkins entered, unhealthily white round the mouth, but still master of himself, the perfect butler under the most disturbing conditions.

"Sir Robert," he announced, "there is some light defect lately arisen in the electric light installation. You may have noticed it yourself, sir. And some of the girls are somewhat alarmed – that is, the younger girls have become needlessly frightened. Perhaps, sir, in the circumstance you would be good enough to favour me with your instructions."

Then Hawkins withdrew, for the lights had begun to flicker, a queer, continuous chattering of breaks in the rays like the flicker of a cinematograph camera. At that new demonstration Hawkins' grip on his jumping nerves gave out. He beat a sudden retreat through the front hall and on to the wide sweep of the stone steps, where already the entire household staff was gathered.

"Quick, Geoffrey, my boy, get out of this! There's some new devilry going on here, and Heaven knows what will happen next. Come on – let's get out of it!"

"Get out? When three hours of rays like these will pulverize the whole house? Where are your main switches?"

"Down in the wine cellars. Right under the house. We'd never locate them with the light like this."

Windermaine made a jump on to the back of a huge armchair. It was under the window. By reaching up he could just manage to grasp the great brass curtain-pole that ran along the top of it. He wrenched it down, a thick, massive thing nearly twelve feet long, with the heavy curtains still hanging on it. He swept them off the rings and stuck one end of the pole into the wide fire grate so that its big brass knob was wedged firmly into the ironwork. The other end reached to the cluster of lights with a few inches to spare.

He propped a chair under the pole to hold it in position, and then with a quick jab he deliberately smashed one of the electric light bulbs, shattering all the glass away from the terminal. A push on the chair jammed the other end of the pole hard up against the broken globe. He had made a powerful short circuit, one strong enough to burn out a thousand fuses in a couple of seconds.

The weird flickering ceased and the glare grew brighter and brighter until the intensity of it blinded the eyes. It reached a pitch of almost savage brilliance, and then one by one the lamps began to burst. They incandesced, blowing out in a white-hot shower of sparks and melted glass. It was happening all over the house. They could hear them fizzing off like siphons of soda. The great curtain pole was glowing with heat.

But the scarifying tingling had ceased and the oppressive load had gone from the air. Only an occasional spurt of sound came from somewhere at the back of the house as the last of the lamps burned out. There was a pungent smell of burning in the air; it was sharp, acrid on the nostrils.

Harrigan pointed to the back of the chair where the pole rested. It was burning the tough old leather and wood. A little spiral of stinging blue smoke was coiling upwards from it. Windermaine waited a few seconds longer and then the main switches blew out a dull, explosive bang that came up sombrely from below. The live-burning glimmering died down on the great pole of brass.

Outside, the voice of Hawkins could be heard calling on some one to get candles and to instal them in all the rooms. His severe, ghostly-looking old face appeared a few moments later holding an elaborate candelabrum over his head. A dozen thin points of light danced wanly on it, but it served to dissipate the shadows.

Harrigan drew in a deep breath of unfeigned relief. "Thank the merciful powers that's over!" he said, shakily. "What on earth was it? How do you account for it?"

"As well ask me what keeps the earth spinning," answered Windermaine in a puzzled voice. "I've no more idea than the man in the moon. But it's obvious that the Horror on the Moor has become executive. Its malignance seems to become centred on Deepvale Manor – for tonight's experiment, anyhow. Somebody – somehow – made use of the wiring system of this house to introduce a new and rather extraordinary force into the house. Not very pleasant to know such things are possible, is it?"

"Indeed not – but—" Harrigan stopped and looked round helplessly. This new departure had shaken him considerably – a good deal more than he would have cared to admit – and he didn't know what to think about it all.

Hawkins placed the candles carefully in the centre of the table and stood back with the barest suspicion of a bow. "With your permission, sir," he said, "I will telephone to the power station at Lynford, acquainting the authorities there with the nature and character of our complaint, requesting at the same time that repairs be put in hand with the utmost despatch."

"Tonight, if possible, Hawkins."

"Very good, Sir Robert."

One of the housemaids came in, white and breathless, to say that after the house had been plunged into final darkness by the blowing out of the fuses she had distinctly seen a white-hot line of fire flash out for a second along the ground all the way from the house to somewhere out on the moor.

"A line of fire?" said Windermaine, hurrying forward. "What was is like – like a thin wire suddenly going blue hot and then fusing?"

The girl nodded. "Yes, sir, that's just about what it *was* like."

"Good! And in which direction was it running?"

"Straight over to Rose Cottage, sir."

"All right, thank you. That will be all."

When the girl had gone, Harrigan turned to him with a fiercely troubled face. "There – what did I tell you?" he snapped. "Do you believe me now?"

"Not once in a thousand years, Sir Robert," replied Windermaine, flatly.

"But I tell you, boy, that woman—"

"My dear friend, if you want me to help you to get at the bottom of this mystery, you must at least extend me the common courtesies. I've already formed my opinion of the tenant of Rose Cottage. And it clashes with yours – clashes at every point in the compass. The very least you can do is to restrain your violent denunciations until such time as you can produce some justification for them."

"Bah!" snorted the baronet. "What's her name, anyway?"

"Rosaine."

"Rosaine nothing. Just that. Her *bona fides* are so absolutely unquestionable that that is the only name she can offer the world; the rest, I presume, is a perfectly innocent silence!"

"Goodnight, sir," said Windermaine coldly.

"What – where are you going, boy?"

"Me?" said Windermaine, swinging round at the door. "I'm going to follow up the trail of that burnt wire!"

"But – but my dear lad! It leads straight to Rose Cottage!"

"Well, what of it?"

"There is death in that house for you!"

"Not death, sir – hope!" said Windermaine, quietly. "And I'm going – now – alone. Goodnight. Whatever dark mystery surrounds Rose Cottage, I shall prove it tonight."

The door clicked and Sir Robert Harrigan was alone.

5

STEALER OF HEARTS

Windermaine groped his way through the darkness up to his room. There were two things he wanted just then: an electric torch – and a gun. He rummaged about among his trunks until he found them.

The torch was harmless enough; but the gun was a Colt, which is about the last word in safety first and last. He fingered it grimly, sixteen ounces of a wicked-looking mixture of blue steel, accuracy, and sudden death. He slid it into his hip-pocket.

Feeling blindly for the wide, polished balustrade, he got downstairs again and slipped out of the front door.

Outside a thin sickle of moon was making fitful appearances through banks of rolling cloud wrack, a wan little gleam of watery light that only intensified the darkness again after it had gone. The clouds were sailing up in great, sullen squadrons out of the black south-west, a sudden wind change that promised a heavy downpour before the night was through.

He flashed his torch along over the thick mould of the garden. It cut a bright little circle of light on the ground, like a tiny searchlight slipping about erratically through the blackness.

In a little while he got on the end of the trail, a thin black line that went snaking away out of the garden towards the moors like a piece of burnt string. He did not wait to find out how the connection to the house had been made – the breakdown party from the power station would do that – but struck away hurriedly in the wake of the trail.

The wire had apparently been laid without any great effort at concealment. Except in the more obviously exposed parts it had merely been strung out along the ground. It coiled over the little knolls and banks and trailed its tenuous length round clumps of undergrowth and gorse. Here and there a little loose earth had been smoothed over it, but so great was the heat of its burning that the traces showed even through the earth.

It appeared that whoever had laid that wire had been expecting to be able to roll it up again quickly and easily before questing eyes had a chance of looking for it. For once out on the open moor all pretence at hiding it was abandoned. The trail showed clear and distinct. Even tough roots of gorse and brush were burned out when the supercharged wire melted.

The moon shone out again for a few seconds. It gave him a clear view for a hundred yards ahead. Straight and true the trail was following the dead line towards Rose Cottage. He hurried forward, switching off his torch to conserve the battery.

Far ahead, about two miles out on the heart of the moor, a tiny light leapt into life – a light in one of the windows of Rose Cottage. He pursed his lips and tried to recall the vision he had seen by the wicket gate earlier in the afternoon, a vision of sweetness and heart-capturing charm, the delightful girl who had taken him softly by the heart-strings without a single conscious effort.

But all he could see was the dominant figure in the great ulster, stalking up the trail of death and into that sweet paradise of Rose Cottage. All he could hear was Harrigan's heated declaration that the great brute had been staying there for years – was, in fact, the actual tenant of the cottage.

And then there was that other faith-shaking knowledge that none of the simple, kindly people round about would have anything to do with Rosaine – that she was an utter outcast, a pariah in their midst. That realisation was devastating, for he knew that, even in little scandal-mongering communities like Deepvale, there is always a little fire to account for the smoke.

He dismissed his thoughts and strode onwards. Then, when he was barging on down a sudden dip in the ground, he stubbed his foot into an unyielding gnarl of roots and went sprawling on his face.

He muttered an oath as he brushed an assortment of gorse spines from his face. "Another good evening suit gone west," he thought, for the thin cloth was torn in a score of half-inch cuts. He fumbled among the underbrush for his torch.

Almost without knowing it, he stiffened into absolute immobility, listening with every atom of pent-up intensity. Slowly he turned his ear to the wind. There were footsteps, heavy, ponderous footsteps, coming rapidly up the trail he himself was following.

He crawled away off the track about ten yards, lifting his knees high over the painful gorse, and then lay flat, drawing his coat up as well as he could to hide the staring whiteness of his dress shirt. Without a sound he slipped his hand back for his gun. There was a thin metallic click as he cocked it. And in the silence, that became more and more electric as the seconds passed, he waited.

The figure loomed into view, tall, black-caped, and sombre. It seemed to overshadow the very ground on which it walked, an automaton, soulless and grim. It stalked past him with a face as set and expressionless as an image carved in rock. The yellow gleam of light fell on the stony features for a few seconds. Motionless, almost unseeing eyes stared out of the black bush of brows and gazed ahead into the darkness as he went stalking by. The skin seemed lifeless, drawn over the high bone of the cheeks as tight as old wash-leather. In the faint radiance of the moon it gleamed like old soapstone. That was as near as Geoffrey Windermaine, or anyone else, had ever got to Carlo Damian since that gloomy omen of evil first came to the moors.

Windermaine was about to rise and follow on in Damian's wake when he heard yet other footfalls stumbling up the track. Unlike Carlo Damian, who went swinging along surefooted as a gorilla, knowing every stick and stone of the ground he strode across, these other footfalls were halting, diffident – the steps of a man nervously unsure of himself.

Windermaine raised himself cautiously and caught sight of a dull white gleam lurching along against the walls of the night.

"Harrigan!" he whispered. "Stop, you fool – that's Damian ahead there!"

The baronet started.

"Heavens, Gerry – you did startle me. I thought I was following *you* – I saw your light."

"What are you doing here?"

"Thought I'd come along and lend a hand. Not right for me to be standing back when there's trouble ahead."

Windermaine said nothing. There was no false sentiment about that young scout of fortune. He was in process of admitting to himself that he was glad to have company out there in the uncanny darkness. The unfathomable mystery of it all was getting on his nerves, leading him to a blank wall beyond which was nothing but the downright supernatural.

"Come on, then," he whispered. "Let's get at it – messing about here is worse than waiting in the dentist's chair. Got a gun?"

Harrigan nodded, and the two pressed forward.

For ten minutes they maintained a tight-lipped silence. Then Windermaine said, "This business is getting a bit too thick for me. I'm going to wire for Standy tomorrow."

"Who's Standy?" asked the baronet.

"Friend of mine – Scotland Yard chap – you'll like him. Solid, reliable sort of fellow; been doing this sort of thing all his life – and he doesn't believe in ghosts. You can't ruffle Standy – just the sort of man we want on a job like this."

"I don't want any nosy detectives ferreting about round Deepvale," snapped the baronet. He didn't admire the unpleasant idea of the law taking a hand in elucidating the mystery that brooded over his ancient home.

"Far better have a detective than no Deepvale" retorted Windermaine. "I'm going to wire for him first thing in the morning, anyhow. This affair seems to me to have possibilities far more serious than we think. Damian's no fool; he's not doing this sort of thing for a hobby. There's something tremendous at the back of all this. He's playing about with forces beyond our conception – playing with them with the dreadful familiarity of a mastermind. The sooner the authorities are acquainted with the facts the better."

"Well, how did you come to know Standy?" asked his host, crossly.

"I've helped him in several jobs up in town. Hobby of mine, amateur detective work. Done quite a lot of it. Had some lucky days, too. Keeps the mind active in spite of a settled income."

Harrigan stumped on in a gloomy silence. He didn't like the idea of it at all. But the job was getting beyond his control – and Windermaine was a masterful young fellow, anyway.

It was a good hour before they got to the wicket gate of Rose Cottage. The light was still burning in the window; it had guided them steadily across the moor; and because of it Windermaine had not had to use his torch.

"Don't touch the gate," he whispered. "He may have some tell-tale wires from it into the house."

Silently they climbed through the gap in the hedge and crawled towards the window. There was no sound from within. All was silent as the grave.

Windermaine peeped in. Rosaine was sitting in an old-fashioned arm-chair in the corner by the fire, reading a book. Now and then she glanced up at the clock and sighed.

"By gosh! Damian hasn't got back yet," said Harrigan. "She's still waiting up from him."

Windermaine clutched his arm to silence him.

"You stay here – keep out of the light of the window," he whispered. "I'm going to the back to have a look round there."

He crept away and in a moment was lost in the darkness.

As he turned the corner of the cottage he thought he heard a slight sound at the front. He stopped and listened, but the silence settled down again, heavy and oppressive. He went forward again.

Far out over the moor the uncanny lights began to flicker, the weird, unearthly lights he had seen when he first came to Deepvale. They stuttered and stammered away, lighting up the close-packed clouds. A few drops of rain began to fall, big, heavy drops that fell dully on the leaves of the laurel bushes.

Greeny-blue the lights were – like summer lightning flickering about among the cloud castles, yet like no lightning he had ever seen in his life. It came upwards from the ground; long, thin-tongued streaks of it, ominously soundless.

"Another devilish stew brewing over there," he muttered, and in that same phrase gave up trying to elucidate the mystery of the lights.

He found himself in a fair-sized kitchen garden with a large outhouse at the far end of it. Stepping high over rows of cabbages, he approached it. Guarding the lens with his hand, he stooped and switched on his torch. The burned-out wire trail went right up to, and under, the door of that outhouse. And from inside came the subdued hum of a whirring machine.

"Not bad, that, for a first-time effort," he said to himself. "Standy couldn't have reasoned it out better."

He tried the door handle gently and pushed it. It yielded to his touch. Gun in one hand, torch in the other, he went in, closed the door behind him, and snapped on his light.

The place was empty save for the humming machine in the corner. It was a long, dynamo-like piece of mechanism, supported on a thick stone slab. What its precise function was he couldn't quite determine in the restricted light his torch threw. But there were shining copper wires all over it and a huge glass tank of mercury. The rotator was revolving at terrific speed, a little chain of blue sparks pouring away steadily from between a pair of carbon terminals.

He looked at his Colt longingly. "You beauty," he mused. "I'd like to put a bullet through the soul of that little lot that would land the whole contraption nicely on the scrap-heap." Then he shook his head. "Too noisy – too noisy by half. Still—"

Without further ado he proceeded to wreck the machine. Systematically and with studied deliberation he went over the thing section by section with a steel wrench. Once he received a terrific shock of electricity, that flung him against the far wall and set up a violent twitching in his muscles. But he went back again doggedly and worked away at the clamps and bolts till the thing began to vibrate noisily on its bearings. Then he aimed a savage, smashing blow at the sputtering carbons.

There was a sudden sheeting of blue-hot flame that scorched the air like the back-draught off a blast furnace, and the whirling rotators began to slow down. In a few seconds they had come to a dead stop, and Windermaine, with his coat off and perspiration standing out in little beads along his forehead, completed his work of destruction.

The rapid vibration had fouled the bearings, strained them out of the true line of the perfect adjustments on which the machine ran. It would take weeks of painstaking work to restore them to their old immaculate precision.

He wrenched away at the great drums, forced apart the shining copper wires, and assaulted the more vulnerable parts with every ounce of strength that was in him. Half an hour's solid, muscle-grinding labour saw the great mechanism a total wreck, smashed beyond all hope of repair. The cleverest mechanic on earth could never have restored it to any semblance of utility again.

Then he crept out, silent as the shadow of an owl across the sky, and went back to where he had left Harrigan on guard. But Harrigan was not there. He called him very softly in the darkness, but there was no reply, only the thin wail of a sea-bird out over the moor where the Channel waves broke on the lonely shore.

"Dashed odd," he muttered, and peeped in through the window. Rosaine was still there, reading, in the chair by the fire. Carlo Damian, apparently, was still abroad on the dripping downs.

He searched all over the great garden, quietly and carefully, going over the ground foot by foot. He hunted among the bushes and all along by the great hedge at the end, but without discovering anything. He sent a call whispering out through the shadows time after time, but no answering whisper came back. He even flashed his torch once or twice to attract attention, but without response. Harrigan was not there.

Windermaine was nettled. He had an unpleasant suspicion that his host had not been able to stand the strain of waiting in the darkness. His nerve had given out and he had turned tail for the warmth and reassurance of Deepvale Manor.

Perhaps the rain, now falling solidly, had been the last straw – and Windermaine admitted, standing there alone in the middle of that dark, ghostly garden, that there is nothing in the whole world of darkness quite so depressing, quite so pregnant with the little pricking devils of fright, as the silent solitudes of the Devon moors round about midnight when the rain is falling warm and heavy on the dead leaves, and the black silhouettes of the hedges and bushes stand out like ghostly, hooded sentinels, keeping guard over legions of unburied dead.

He waited a few minutes longer, soaked to the skin, hoping against hope for some sign of Harrigan. Slowly he found himself straining his ears into the silence. From Heartsmeet Lane he heard the sinister footfalls again, the unmistakable, undisguisable, striding footsteps of Carlo Damian, coming back to his cottage. He made no attempt at caution, spurned even to muffle his heavy boots.

Up the lane and in through the gate he came, turning those baleful eyes neither to the right nor the left, a seven-foot giant of a man who, in some immense way, seemed to regard the rest of humanity as mere groundlings, pygmies beneath the notice of his monumental brain.

He opened the door with a key. "So he's got his own key, has he?" whispered Windermaine savagely as the door slammed. He crept back to the window and looked in cautiously. The sight he saw inside sent a hot surge of sullen anger sweeping through him. Rosaine, the girl he had already throned in his soul on a pedestal of gold, the girl who, in one short half-hour, had snared his heart in a witchery of silver chains, was in his arms, gladly, eagerly, her own arms round his neck, printing kisses on his great leather-skinned lips.

To Windermaine there was something altogether repulsive in the way the great mouth split into a smile – a smile was the last thing on earth one would associate with a mouth like that; it was like listening to grand opera pouring from the throat of an enormous baboon. He was fondling her hair, touching her shoulders with his immense hands.

Windermaine turned away from the window with a feeling of disgust and utter chagrin in his soul. He was thankful at that moment for one single thing; and that was that self-opinionated old Sir Robert Harrigan was not there to come jumping in with his "I told you so." That phrase would have been inevitable after all that had passed; and of all phrases on earth it is the bitterest and most exasperating to one whom Fate has mocked with a broken faith.

Careless of the noise he made, he went back down the path through the garden and out into the rain-soaked ways of Heartsmeet. The water was squelching dismally in his light evening shoes and he was thoroughly wet and miserable. He was out of temper with himself. Six hours before he was ready to stake his life on the innocence and sweetness of that girl who, even at that moment, was in the arms of what was practically an ogre. He was hurt in his pride – hurt to the very quick of his finer feelings.

It was a beastly walk back to Deepvale. His garments hung about him, clammy and cold where the driving rain beat against him. He felt that for two pins he would have walked all the way back to Rose Cottage and shot that leering brute where he stood, shot him without a pang or a regret.

It was in that frame of mind, and just as he was turning into the drive leading up to the Manor, that he stumbled over an obstacle in the pathway.

"Confound!" he muttered, rubbing a nastily skinned knee. He swished his torch round. A throaty moan came from just behind him and he wheeled round with a startled gasp. The torch swung across and illuminated the prone figure of a man, flat on his face in the driveway. He was trussed up hand and foot and a handkerchief was tied tightly round his mouth. There was thick peat mud all over him, but the cut of the clothes was obvious at first glance. It was Harrigan.

He was bound with strong wire drawn so tightly as to be almost cutting the flesh; and there was a savage-looking wound at the base of his skull.

Windermaine had no knife with him, but he did his best with a small pair of nail scissors. Having forced the shears through a few of the strands, he managed to get the remainder off; and with a heave he hoisted the baronet on his back and carried him in.

Harrigan was unconscious, and remained so all night, unable to give any explanation as to how he came to be in that extraordinary condition. A doctor was sent for from Lynford, but was not expected until early in the morning at the very least. So the old housekeeper sat up with him, with a footman, armed with a rifle, in case an emergency should arise.

Windermaine, tired and feeling sick with himself turned into bed and slept like a log.

6

THE GIRL FROM ROSE COTTAGE

The light of the dawn broke cold and pale. The weather had cleared a little; the rain had ceased, but laden clouds still marched slowly across the sky, looking as though they were only seeking a likely spot to halt and begin emptying themselves again.

Eight o'clock brought the doctor and a telegram from Valerie to say that she had caught the midnight boat from Calais and would be in Deepvale by midday.

The doctor shook his head and looked serious. Windermaine was with him, in dressing-gown and slippers. Privately, and in a very guarded way, he gave the doctor a *résumé* of the events of the previous night. The doctor seemed shocked and not a little incredulous. "But," as he said, "it's none of my affair. I can't do anything until he regains consciousness. The wound is clean, thanks to the housekeeper, and he seems fairly comfortable. On that I hazard the presumption that there will be no further complications. But he has had a terrible blow."

"How long is he likely to remain unconscious?" asked Windermaine.

The doctor shrugged his shoulders.

"In a case like this, it's almost impossible to say," he said. "He may come round at any minute. On the other hand, it may be hours, or even days, before consciousness returns. I've known cases of severe concussion where the patient has remained almost comatose for twenty days. But in those cases the brain was injured – or there was some other serious complication already existing before the concussion occurred. In this case I don't think there is. The brain, at least, appears to me to be uninjured."

Windermaine nodded.

"You will stay, of course?"

"Naturally. Sir Robert is a personal friend of mine. I will remain all day, if necessary."

Windermaine turned down the coverlet and looked at the baronet's hands. There were deep red weals all over them where he had rubbed them the previous night, and some of the skin had scaled off.

The doctor stared at them through a pair of glasses.

"How did that happen?" he inquired.

Windermaine told him and showed him that his own hands were equally savaged by the burning rays.

Together they made a tour of the house and the doctor confessed himself utterly baffled. In every room where the lights had been turned on, the wallpaper was badly faded and discoloured. Some of the carpets and rugs had been almost bleached. And there was a film of roughness over the polished furniture, almost as though the woodwork had been subjected to a vigorous sandpapering. Certain fabrics, such as silk and *crêpe-de-Chine*, had rotted so that they fell apart at a touch.

An oddity was that all the mirrors had been rendered useless, the quicksilver having apparently evaporated, leaving only the dull red lacquer composition at the back. Glass and metals were unharmed, but newspapers had turned yellow as though with age.

"Extraordinary," muttered the doctor. "I've no theory to account for it. I'll really have to go closer into this."

Windermaine left him to his ruminations and went up to dress.

Twelve o'clock brought no change in the condition of Harrigan, and Windermaine realised that he was in the incomfortable predicament of having to play deputy for his own host to the girl whom both his father and her father had every intention of him marrying. It was difficult, and thoroughly unorthodox, to say the least.

Valerie he had not seen for two years. She was rather gawky then. No, not gawky – Valerie was never that – but unfinished, loose-endy, not quite sure of herself. Now he came to think of it, she certainly had always been very nice to him. She had the happy knack of remembering special, intimate dates, and the postman always brought him some charming little remembrancer of the occasion.

Italy would have finished her as not even France could have done. Paris goes too far with its methods; having sharpened to perfection, it is apt to blunt. The finished product of the gay city is more than a little blasé.

But Italy should have touched her with a light, understanding hand. After Florence, Rome, Venice, and Milan, Valerie should be more than worthy of respectful interest. And after last night at Rose Cottage....

A car had gone to Lynford to fetch her. He fell to wondering how long it would be. He was rather looking forward to that meeting with Valerie – it wasn't going to be half as difficult as he had imagined. Awkward at first, of course, while he was breaking the news about her father, but that would give him breathing time. A horn sounded in the grey distance.

He stepped over to the window. Yes, sure enough, there was the car, piled high with trunks and portmanteaux.

The door opened and he turned. Hawkins, grave and dignified as ever, despite his mission, entered and paused a few paces inside.

"A lady, who gives the name of Miss Rosaine, wishes to see you, sir," he announced. "She is in the library and seems very agitated – she begged me to tell you that the matter is of extreme urgency."

Windermaine stared at Hawkins's stolid old face as though his brain couldn't quite make definite contact with the statement. He was trying to comprehend the greater significance of the butler's story.

"What – *what?*" he said.

Hawkins, with ponderous aloofness, repeated the message.

Then the impossibility of the situation swept across him with a rush. Rosaine, the girl of a million dreams, but now a nightmare apparition – waiting for him in the library. Valerie, the girl he had never even thought to consider until that morning, the girl he had simply accepted as a mere entity among his myriad acquaintances, but who was now the centre of his interest – rapidly nearing the house in the car.

There were less than ten desperate seconds left to him in which to think out the right course of action.

Rosaine had come to him openly. The butler knew it. Doubtless other of the servants were aware of her presence by now. It was a matter he could not possibly mask from Harrigan. The baronet would come to hear of it within a few hours of stirring to consciousness. Rosaine, the siren, in his house, under his noble old roof!

After his wild outburst against the "beautiful witch" there was not the slightest doubt as to how he would take it.

What on earth had made her do it? And with Valerie there, too! The situation became more highly charged with every new consideration that jangled into his brain. The girl must either be a fool or the wickedest, deeply-scheming creature on earth.

Windermaine knew she was not blind to the vilification the old diehard of Deepvale heaped upon her. It was she herself who had told him all about it. She knew exactly what Sir Robert thought of her.

And yet, on the face of it, there must be some vital reason for her reckless visit. Windermaine jumped to the hope that she might even know something about the murderous attack on Sir Robert. Somebody held the explanation to that mystery. And it might be as well the girl as anyone else on the moors.

In that case his duty was to see her first – obviously the two could not be allowed to meet. Her information might be of the utmost assistance to him when the time came for him to face Valerie and make his explanations.

Having reduced the question to something approaching a logical answer, he made up his mind quickly.

"All right, Hawkins, I'll see her," he said. "Miss Valerie is just arriving? Tell her I will see her the moment I am free, and that I am engaged for a moment with a visitor. You need not mention names. And please do not speak of this matter in the presence of Sir Robert. At least, not for a day or two."

He went into the library as the bell pealed in the entrance hall. Rosaine rose to meet him as he closed the door. He looked at her quickly and was disturbed at the sudden change in her. The sweet violet eyes had lost their merry flash; the impish fun was no longer peeping out of them. They were anxious, harassed; almost the glitter of fear was burning in them.

And she was white-faced, too. The soft pink of roses had drained away; she looked utterly weary. Her boots were soddened with water – definite proof that she had come all the way through the wet heather on foot.

"Well?" said Windermaine.

He could be very politely icy when he chose; and the single word fell like a crackling icicle.

She hurried over to him, and stood in front of him, her face upturned to his, nervous, distracted.

"Mr Windermaine," she said, breathlessly, "you must excuse me for coming to you here – I would never have allowed even my shadow to pollute the home of Sir Robert Harrigan had the circumstances been other then they are, but—"

"There is no need to prolong your apologies," broke in Windermaine, curtly. "You are here and there's an end of it. Perhaps you will explain."

Rosaine went a shade whiter, hurt beyond words at his tone. She looked at him weakly for a moment and tried to collect her jumping thoughts.

"*Why* have you come here?" there were steel daggers sticking out among the words.

"Mr Windermaine – I've come to warn you," she said with a rush.

"For that I owe you my very grave thanks – but it still leaves its own question unexplained, does it not?"

"You must – you must go away from here. There is grave danger threatening you – and I beg of you, oh, I beg of you, to go right away – today – now – don't even stop to pack."

The words came tumbling out of her mouth in a breakneck stream.

Her mouth, that dainty, kissable mouth, was trembling with agitation, and she was screwing her handkerchief to a ball in her fingers.

"Indeed" said Windermaine coldly. "And now will you please be good enough to explain exactly what you mean by this extraordinary presumption?"

"No, no! I cannot! All I can do is to beg of you to leave Deepvale, to get right out of Devon. Lose yourself, don't go near your own haunts, get right away where you will not be known and where even your friends cannot trace you. Oh, please listen to me and believe me when I tell you that you are standing in the midst of a terrible danger."

"Not much more than St. George's Day on the Zeebrugge Mole, I hope?"

"Please – please, Mr, Windermaine, don't make fun of me!" she burst out. "The danger is very real. It is all round you at every moment of the day, and you cannot evade it. Oh, won't you *please* listen to me?"

"Miss Rosaine," said Windermaine, firmly, "there is no danger so terrible that it may not be named. If you will tell me exactly what this matter is I will at least discuss it with you. But if you persist in talking in riddles, I'm afraid I must ask you to go. You are aware, of course, that you are laying yourself open to grave suspicion?"

"But I'm not – I—"

"Yes, you are! You surely know that Sir Robert Harrigan is lying seriously ill upstairs?"

"Yes, yes. I know he is."

"And that he is still unconscious from a savage blow on the skull?"

"Yes – please! – it was about that that I have come to see you!"

"And that, up to the present, there is not the smallest knowledge as to what happened; not the faintest explanation to the mystery? You see what I'm driving at? Sir Robert Harrigan is found half dead outside his own house, in the pouring rain at midnight. He is bound and gagged; at his last gasp. I know, because I found him.

"The last that was seen of him was outside your cottage window, an hour and a half earlier in the night. I know, because I was there with him. You were sitting in a chair by the fire, reading, wearing the dress you're wearing now except that you had brown shoes on instead of black boots. Is that right? Very well, I think you'll admit I was actually there. You now come to me with a lot of half-hysterical warnings, begging me to clear out of Deepvale unless I want something equally dreadful to happen to me. And yet you say you are not laying yourself open to suspicion?"

Rosaine was looking at him through horror-filled eyes.

"Mr Windermaine," she gasped, "you surely don't think I wounded Sir Robert?"

"No. Neither do I think you had any hand at all in the disgraceful outrage. But at the same time I certainly do declare that your conduct has been quite sufficient to justify even the slowest-brained village constable on earth arresting you on suspicion. And also for presuming that you know a great deal more than you care to tell. To an honest woman there is only one obvious way out of your present predicament – and that is to tell the full story as you know it, hiding nothing, withholding nothing."

The girl looked helplessly round the great room, bewildered, dismayed. That cold, aggressive reception was the last thing she had expected from Windermaine. He was forcing his dominance on her, pressing her into a trap of her own making. She felt the very ground slipping from under her feet.

The realisation of Windermaine's complete change of attitude towards her left her feeling stunned. There was a hunted look in her eyes and the handkerchief was being pulled to rags. And the greatest shock of all was the knowledge that Windermaine was at Rose Cottage with Harrigan. That was a piece of information that knocked her world off its balance.

Windermaine went on inexorably:—

"Let me explain further. Last night an attempt was made to destroy this house. Only the fact that I have some faint glimmerings of scientific knowledge saved this beautiful mansion from complete annihilation. The method employed was too technical and too utterly unique for me to be able to tell you how it was done. I don't know myself. I have only the barest inkling of the principles employed. But the attempt failed, chiefly owing to the fact that I was able to blow the fuses out.

"A few minutes later the remnant of a burn-out wire was discovered, running in a direct line from this house to Rose Cottage. That wire found connections in the electric wiring system at this end – and in an outhouse behind Rose Cottage at the other!"

He watched her intently as he tabled his evidence, item after item of solid fact that was slowly condemning her where she stood. There was livid fear in her eyes, the desperate fear of an animal that finds itself driven into a corner, with every way of escape closing down about it.

"Miss Rosaine, I'm being perfectly fair to you," he went on. "I'm telling you just a little of what I know. Only a little. I assure you I know a great deal more – information that I am reserving until the arrival of the police."

At that last word a quick cry of alarm broke from her lips.

"The police! Ah, no, please, Mr Windermaine, for the love of pity don't bring the police into this!"

"Scotland Yard has already been given a fair outline of the facts," replied Windermaine, with steely incisiveness. "I had a long conversation with the head of the Criminal Investigation Department myself on the long-distance wire this morning. A detective is coming down now by fast car – he will be here within two hours.

"If you've nothing to be afraid of, why are you so terrified at the thought of police intervention? You surely realise your position? Even if I don't tell him, that detective will find the. trail of that wire and will be knocking at your door within thirty minutes of getting his eyes on it. Why not come out into the open and tell me what you know?"

She looked at him beseechingly.

"Oh, Mr Windermaine, won't you please believe me?" she pleaded. "I am not hiding anything for my own sake. I am risking my life here for yours. I swear I am not responsible for the things you've discovered. I am only here to warn you. Please don't cross-examine me like this. I cannot tell you what you want to know. All I ask of you is to go away – to go away and forget all about Deepvale and the moors – and me."

"May I ask why you have come here to warn me?"

Tears were streaming down her cheeks, hot tears falling like spilling dew from the wet wood-violets.

"Only because you were decent to me – you were nice to me, friendly on sight. And – Heavens, it was so wonderful to find a friend in this slanderous place. I thought I had found someone at last who would take me on trust – but even you have changed. Your manner to me is like that of the rest of them. And still I want to think of you as you were to me yesterday, kind, understanding, a sympathetic fellow-creature. I want you to go away – as far as you can from this accursed place."

Windermaine took her by the shoulders and made her sit down.

"Now," he said, quietly but firmly, "let's have an end of this word fencing. Time is slipping away, precious minutes that you may regret to the end of your life. I don't want you to think me brutal – or even unjust; but get to the bottom of this mystery I will. And I'm giving you a last chance. Think over this carefully and you will realise what a hopeless situation you are creating for yourself. Last night Sir Robert Harrigan and I arrived outside Rose Cottage about ten o'clock."

Rosaine looked up fearfully.

"Well?" she whispered.

"Carlo Damian was walking ahead of us all the way."

The girl gasped. Windermaine pretended not to have noticed. "I was creeping round to the back of the house when I heard a faint noise – it might have been the sound of a violent blow at the back of an unsuspecting head and the soft flop of a body falling. I say it might have been. It sounded very much like that. I got back half an hour later. Sir Robert Harrigan was nowhere to be found. He had gone; vanished like a puff of smoke.

"For over half an hour I hunted and harried among the bushes and hedges around. There was not a yard of that great garden I did not search. But – Harrigan was not there. Just as I was preparing to go I heard the sound of footsteps coming back up the lane. It was Carlo Damian.

"Something over an hour had elapsed since we trailed Damian to your cottage – an hour, that is, since I heard that sound of a body falling. That would have been just about sufficient time for him to have made that double journey, wouldn't it? From your window to Deepvale Manor and back. Just about an hour's walk for a man who knew every tuft of grass on the way. I think, if I advise the detective to put Damian under immediate arrest, we shall have more than half solved the mystery of the attack on Harrigan, don't you?"

But Rosaine did not answer. She had broken down. With her head in her arms on the table she was sobbing helplessly, giving way to a pent-up storm of despair.

Windermaine touched her very gently.

"Won't you tell me now?" he asked. "You must see that you cannot hide the truth from the authorities longer than a few hours. And by your silence you are only heaping up a mountain of dreadful trouble for yourself. I know perfectly well that you yourself are innocent – at least, in this Harrigan affair – and that you are merely trying to shield someone. And that that someone is Carlo Damian. You have failed even to avert suspicion from him. His guilt is as obvious as your emotion. Why continue fighting a battle you have already lost?"

The sobbing shook her slim body and she could not answer.

Windermaine sent down his final barrage.

"Little girl," he said, "I have seen things down here which well-nigh surpass belief. I have seen a great wild swan collapse in a welter of broken bones and mutilated flesh – in mid-air. I have seen a running hare knocked spinning into death without a sound being heard.

"I have seen a trail of utter annihilation drawn across the moors from one skyline to the other – a trail that withered the very earth in its wake. Nothing will ever grow in that streak again from now till the crack of doom. The very life of the soil, the essence that gives nourishment to seeds and all growing things, has been obliterated from it.

"I have seen the skin peeling off my hands before my eyes – at the behest of a disintegrating blue ray forced into the electric-lighting installation of this very house. And, impossible as it sounds, I *know* that all these things are merely symptoms, a mere peppering of experiments in preparation for something of far greater significance.

"The real horrors are yet to come. They are being prepared and perfected, slowly but surely, in the brain of that devil in human form, Carlo Damian. And your action in trying to shield him makes your own position absolutely untenable. You cannot maintain it any longer.

"Damian does not stand one chance in a million of putting his nightmare schemes into operation. Scotland Yard will have got him by the throat before the night is out. We know where to look for him. Out there on the moors – when the green lights flash. Rosaine, there will be fifty – a hundred men, if necessary – strung out there among the downs, watching every yard of the moors, until they have run Damian to his lair. Now, won't you be sensible and tell? There can be no sitting on the fence in so terrible a matter as this. Either you are on the side of law and order – or you are with Damian and all his horrors. Come along now, which is it?"

7

THE MAN WHO OVERHEARD

Rosaine slowly sat up and faced him. She was making a great effort to control herself, but her eyes were streaming. Windermaine's relentless exposition as much as his dogged purposefulness had crowded out her own tenacity. She was beaten by the picture of the net he had painted around her.

"I'll – I'll tell you," she said, hopelessly. "I'll tell you as much as I dare. Damian would kill me if he knew I had come here – kill me with as little compunction as he would you."

Windermaine nodded.

"He is the terrible danger which, according to you, is threatening me wherever I go, isn't he? He's the danger you want me to run away from?"

"Yes – but you are mocking me again. You don't know his power. It is awful, frightful. Sometimes I think I shall go mad. I believe I *am* going mad. I can't stand the strain of it much longer. He swore last night that he would make his first human experiment on you."

"Charming thought," commented Windermaine.

"Something went wrong with his plans last night. He thought it was Harrigan who had done it. Then when he got back he found one of his machines broken beyond all hope of repair – a chaos of torn and broken parts. He'd spent five years perfecting that machine. It creates a force that can be transmitted along a wire, like electricity. A new invention in the world of science – a tremendous achievement

"But this is only one of his horrible inventions. The others are far greater, far more dreadful. That one was merely a toy. And you broke it. He nearly went mad. He knew it was you. It couldn't have been Harrigan. His rage was awful to watch. He was nearly demented. I believe if he had had you in his hands he would have torn you in pieces. That is why I came to you. You have no idea of his power. He can strike you dead without coming anywhere within miles of you."

"Thank you," said Windermaine, very stiffly. "And what else?"

"Don't try to find him – please, for my sake. It's no use coming to Rose Cottage for him. He's gone. He went last night, in a white heat of passion, after coming back from the outhouse. Before he went he said he would never be coming back to Rose Cottage. He has gone off for the last time. What is going to happen next I dare not think."

"I dare," said Windermaine, grimly. "We are going out tonight to scour the downs. We shall stay out, night after night, until we get him."

"Mr Windermaine," said the girl, earnestly, "I tell you in all sincerity that you will never succeed. He will trap you as easily and as horribly as he has trapped others who have gone out there ferreting about. He is responsible for every mysterious disappearance that has happened on the moors since he first got his great machines into motion. You can send a thousand men out to search for him if you wish. You will be sending them out to their doom. You'll be murdering them. For they will never come back. You'll not even know how they died or at what point they vanished."

"And is that all?"

"Yes. I've said too much already. I dare not tell you more."

"Where does Damian hide on the moors?"

"I don't know," she answered, quietly, and Windermaine knew she was not telling the truth.

"If I brought you a map of the district, could you point out the spot – or near-abouts?" he persisted.

The hunted, frightened look shot back into her face and her eyes began questing round the room again. But after a little while, and with a very white face, she faltered:

"Yes, I – I think so."

"There's just one more question before you go. Why are you shielding Carlo Damian?"

She looked away and a shudder ran through her.

"Come now, there must be a reason," he coaxed. "Surely you wouldn't be foolish enough to say it's for love of him. He is mad. You realise that. Everybody in the district knows it. A stark, staring lunatic, with heaven alone knows what ghastly ideas at the back of his demented brain. Yet you persist in making excuses for him. You shelter him and speak of him as though he were in the right and we were in the wrong. Why? What is the reason behind it all?"

Rosaine was silent for a long time. Then, after glancing at him once or twice, she said:

"I'd like a few minutes to think that over, Mr Windermaine, if you would be kind enough to permit me. There are several things to be considered, and – and, candidly, I'd like to think them over quietly."

"Very well; that's perfectly fair. I'll go and get that map. There's a large one in the old chest in the hall."

He turned and went over to the door, turned as though to speak to her again, thought better of it, and went out. As he pulled the door open, a man, who had been kneeling with his ear to the keyhole, hurriedly shot upright and jumped back.

Windermaine jerked the door to behind him.

"Standy!" he muttered. "Good heavens, man – when did you get here?"

"Headquarters came through to me on the 'phone a couple of hours ago. I was in Taunton, finishing off a little job – nothing much. The Chief himself was on the line. Seemed all hot over your order – gave me a brief outline of the case as he'd heard it from you, and I got on the car right away."

Windermaine took him by the arm and steered him across to the hall.

"Not too loud, old man," he said. "I'm dashed glad to see you, anyway. It looks to me as though we have run our heads into about as big a job as the Yard has ever been called upon to handle. You'll think so, too, when you get the whole hang of it. There's more dark devilry going on round here than ever was brewed in the witches' cauldron."

Standy eyed him squarely. He was a shortish, stocky little man in a big tweed coat that smelt as strongly of tobacco as an old pipe. He carried an air of forceful authority – it was sticking out all over him from the top of his bowler hat to the caps of his thick boots. There was nothing shifty about him.

He stared hard at you, almost rudely, and so far as he was concerned there were only two types of human beings on earth – "straight" and "crooked." The straights could look after themselves, but it was his mission in life to look after the crookeds in person.

Rather small eyes that rarely smiled, hair going thin on the top, a nose that had been broken in a rough-house flare-up down in dockland, a sandy moustace clipped short, a smoothly rounded, boyish-looking chin, and the voice of a hard-case first mate. That was Standy, of the C.I.D., New Scotland Yard.

"I'm arranging for you to have lunch with me privately," said Windermaine. "I can give you the whole story then – every fact I've been able to lay my hands on. You'll probably want help from headquarters."

"Well, *you* don't seem to have been letting the grass grow under your feet, anyway," said Standy.

"What do you mean – about that girl in there?"

"Yes, I heard pretty well all you said. You seem to have got a mighty good grip of the case as it is. You certainly know where to go for the facts. How did you get hold of her? She's going to be useful. Pity you let her get away."

Windermaine blinked and looked at the detective oddly.

"Get away?" he said. "I'm afraid I don't quite get you, Standy. She's in there, waiting for me."

Standy chuckled to himself and hung up his hat.

"Oh, no," he said, gently. "You've got a lot to learn yet – about that sex, anyway. She got rid of you like falling off a log. Got rid of you, boy. Easy. Sent you out for a map like a good little boy. French windows in that room, aren't there? Noticed 'em as we drove up. Bad defect of the whole house. All the ground-floor windows open inward. She's gone. Take a look and see."

Windermaine did. He was across the hall and in through the library door again with a jump. And the great room was empty. The high French windows stood open and the wind was blowing the curtains about. But there was no Rosaine. Outside was a single footmark on the brown earth of the flower border. But that was all. She herself was gone. And Windermaine knew it would be futile to set off in pursuit. On those great lonely spaces she could play hide-and-seek with him, she who knew as much about the moors as did Carlo Damian himself.

"Damn!" he said, and stood glaring out over the rain-soaked landscape. He wouldn't have minded being tricked by the girl, for, despite his attitude to her that morning, he still had his own private opinion of Rosaine. But she had made him lose face before Standy, and that was a bit annoying.

He was going back to the Yard man when there was a sudden commotion on the stairs. Somebody was running down, calling him urgently by name. He ran out and met the doctor, white-faced and agitated.

"Quick, Mr Windermaine!" he said. "Sir Robert Harrigan is dying! A relapse has set in and he is sinking fast. His daughter is up there with him. He wants to see you and Valerie alone before he goes. Don't wait for me. Hurry! He has but a few minutes to live."

8

HER VOW OF LOVE

Shocked beyond measure, Windermaine turned and raced for the stairs. Tragedy seemed to be piling on tragedy in that house of dread. He hurried to the bedroom, and there he found the old baronet propped up in bed; it was plain that the end was very near.

Valerie was barely visible from the bedside. She was half sitting, half lying on a wide divan by the window, her face buried in the cushions, weeping unrestrainedly, but with the dreadful silence of the heartbroken. Windermaine felt a tug in his own heart as he saw her sitting there.

Gerry bent his head. The baronet's lips were moving, but the words were barely audible.

"Hard – hard for the girl, Geoffrey," he said, and his eyes burned their deeper meaning into the younger man. "I'm going. Going fast. Pity I couldn't have lived to – to see you two happy together. You've got to face it now, boy. In a minute she will be all alone in the world. Her – her mother went just – just as suddenly as this. There's no one left – no one I can trust – to look after her. She's yours, boy. Promised to you since your own dad died. I promised him that when I was standing where you are now – straining my ears to catch his last words. You hear me, boy?"

"Yes. Tell me – did Damian do this?"

Harrigan was making a gigantic fight for it. The intensity of it showed in the strained lines of the jaws and the fingers drumming a twitching tattoo on the bed-cover.

"Yes. Careful – how you handle him. Strength of a dray-horse. Took my face in his hands and bashed my head on the fence. Valerie with you? Where are you, boy? I – I can't see! Quick, Geoffrey – get her – I'm going!"

"Miss Harrigan!" called Geoffrey, sharply.

She ran to the bedside, her face, blinded with tears, turned away from Gerry.

"Valerie – is that you, little girl?"

She squeezed the fluttering hand. The door opened and the doctor hurried in, his arms full of great ice compresses.

"Promise me – you know what I mean – you'll be good to him. Promise me."

The girl poured out her heart to him, clinging to his neck, sobbing out a torrent of promises and assurances that sprang from her, unchecked, in an endearing stream.

Windermaine, with a quick gesture, motioned the doctor back. He had seen what was hidden from the surgeon; the sudden, abrupt dulling of the eyes and the single twitch that shivered through the frame as the fingers ceased their drumming. The last little trickle of the sands had run out. The ancient line of the Harrigans was ended.

Gerry tiptoed out of the room. He closed the door behind him and almost ran down the stairs, leaving the doctor to his ministrations and the girl to her grief.

He went into the library, mopping the perspiration from his brow. That had been the most horrible five minutes of his life.

Standy was waiting for him there, stolid, practical, the embodiment of the man to whom affliction is part of the daily round. He looked up with half-raised eyebrows.

"All over?" he inquired.

"Yes," said Gerry, and shut his eyes in an effort to banish the memory of the scene he had just left.

"That makes it murder, then," muttered the detective, and some would have said there was an underlying note of quiet satisfaction in the utterance. "Here's where Carlo Damian unbuttons his collar for the long drop. Well, if you ask my candid opinion, I'd say it's better to have a brute like Damian on the rope than in Dartmoor. Safer to make a real job of it while you're at it."

He made a few careful entries in his notebook, pulling out a heavy silver watch to confirm the time on the library clock. Then he looked shrewdly at Gerry.

"You look as though you've had a tough five minutes, my son," he said.

"Tough!" echoed Windermaine. "Standy, it was awful! I've just had to stand and listen to a heartbroken girl promise to marry me!"

"Eh?"

"Harrigan was so far gone he could scarcely see. The girl was nearly prostrate. I thought she was going to collapse. But he made her go through with it. A death-bed oath!" He mopped his forehead again. "How she saw it through, Heaven knows. If it had lasted any longer I should have cracked up myself."

Standy licked the end of his pencil.

"Well, what's wrong? Don't you want to marry her?" he said.

"Marry her? Why, I haven't even seen her for two years. I haven't even *seen* her now. She didn't look at me. I don't even know what she's like. Girls alter so much from twenty-one to twenty-three. Besides, it isn't what I want at all. Man alive, that sort of thing is for *her* to decide, not me. It's her choice. Harrigan has had that particular bee in his bonnet for years, regardless of Valerie's ideas on the subject. And he forced it on her on his deathbed. Why, the poor girl was nearly distracted.

She can't have known what she was saying. No one but a monster would dream of holding her to a promise like that!"

"Well, step in and tell her what you think about it."

"Don't be an idiot. It will be days before I can even hint at such a distressing matter. Shake yourself. Try to climb out of that police-court groove. Think of the position. She comes home after two years' absence abroad to find the whole house walking about on tiptoe, nobody to welcome her except the servants. Her father is upstairs, apparently pulling round after a murderous attack by a lunatic. The butler informs her that I am a guest in the house. I don't even get the chance to see her or explain how the accident happened. So far as she can understand, I am deliberately giving her the cold shoulder – ignoring her.

"Her father has a sudden and totally unexpected relapse. We are both called to the bedside, and before she knows it she is promising a dying man to marry me and to make me the happiest man on earth! And you tell me to step in and tell her what I think about it. Standy, you're either daft or the most callous, bloodless, stone image that ever happened on earth."

Standy seemed slightly surprised.

"Referring to the matter that occasions my presence here," he said, smoothly, "where is Rose Cottage? I think I ought to go along and see this little Rosaine. Ought to be profitable."

Windermaine pulled himself up with a jerk. Rose Cottage! That was another consideration that had to be taken into account in this bewildering whirl of events.

Yesterday he had promised to see Rosaine, there in Heartsmeet, at four o'clock. He had deliberately chosen the time, too – four o'clock, that being the time of Valerie's expected arrival at Deepvale Manor. He could remember his words at parting. "I shall be there, Rosaine – and I shall be disappointed if you are not." Dear, delicious moment, with the sun shining in his soul and his heart alive with all the little wonder-songs that only sing to a man once in his life.

And Rosaine had said, "Tomorrow, perhaps, you may not be so pleased to see me!"

"Phew!" he muttered. "Was ever a man in such a hopeless mess?"

To Windermaine, with death in the house, it was little short of sacrilege to talk or even think of other things. But the mills of the law grind on though nations fall and empires perish. And the law decrees that when a man is murdered his murderer shall hang. Furthermore, it ordains that the murderer shall not remain at liberty for one second longer than circumstances compel. Standy was waiting for him, his pencil between his teeth.

Windermaine faced his friend frankly.

"Look here, Standy," he said, "I don't want you to go near Rose Cottage until" – he paused in some slight confusion – "well, until later on – say, after sunset."

"What's the idea? Want to give her every chance of getting away with it?"

Windermaine coloured.

"No," he said, "not that at all. But I – dash it all, Standy, I know you've got every right and justification for arresting her on suspicion – you can take her for being an accomplice – for being an accessory both before and after – and for any one of half a dozen things, shielding Damian among them. I know you've a case against her and that you're itching to get her under arrest, but—"

Gerry stopped and his colour increased. He saw that Standy was near to laughing at him.

"Me? Arrest *her*?" he said, derisively. "My lad, you want a cold shower. Gosh! I wouldn't arrest that kid. You seem to have mislaid your thinking-cap. Don't you realise she's the one living link between us and the man we want? So long as she's out and about she's telling us things about Damian. She might not know it, but she is. Leastways, she's telling 'em to me; you don't seem to be so lucky. Oh, no, Mr Windermaine, that girl stays up above ground. Sooner or later she will lead us right up to the man we're after. But I'd like to see her all the same."

"Why?"

"She knows how many beans make five. Over and above which she's straight, straight as a plumb-line. All the time you were hammering at her just now she only told you one lie – and it stuck out a mile! She knows where Damian goes to earth all right. And sooner or later we'll get him, through her."

"Any objection to me being there?"

Standy looked at him hard, his little sandy moustache sticking out like a row of bristles.

"Like that, eh?" he said bluntly. "Well, congratulations, son. You've picked a real one. Reckon I know now why the complication upstairs is giving you brain fever. Still, that's your medicine – nothing to do with me. My experience of life is that there isn't a crime on the calendar but what there's a woman in it, at both ends and in the middle. I make it a rule of life never to get mixed up in that particular section of it. What time do you want to see her?"

"Four o'clock."

"This afternoon?"

"Yes."

"Never said anything about it while I was blocking up that keyhole."

"Possibly not. I made the appointment yesterday."

"Oh!" said Standy, and half closed his eyes. "Going to be a bit difficult – after this morning," he hazarded.

"Devilish. But I shall be there."

"At four o'clock?"

"At four precisely."

"I'll be along about five."

"Thank you. You'll find Rose Cottage up the main road and then about a mile farther on over the downs on the right. Can't mistake it. Two miles away, all told; up a little lane called Heartsmeet."

"Sounds like a film title, doesn't it?" grunted Standy.

9

THE MYSTERY OF BLACK DEEP

Windermaine was fated never to keep that appointment. Not that the breaking of it was anything he could have circumvented, for, like bargains, it takes two to make an appointment, and Rose Cottage, when he went there that afternoon, was empty.

The heavy rain clouds had either emptied themselves dry or sailed away northward when he set out with Mack on his heels.

He reached Heartsmeet with a minute or two to spare, and hung about, waiting for Rosaine. She did not come and he grew impatient. Gerry had said nothing about going up to the door – "here at the wicket gate" was the compact they made – and he waited on and on as the minutes dragged by. Mack, scenting something that held promise of a little higher excitement later on, snuffled his way along the hedge with tail wagging.

There was a great silence. It seemed as though the very birds had ceased their twittering. Mists hung away to seaward and rolled like wisps of torn vapour over the tops of the higher downs.

Windermaine sat on the side of the gate and smoked away at his pipe. Not a sound came from Rose Cottage; it had a vacant, tenantless look – almost as though something of the desolate emptiness of the country around had crept inside it and taken up its solitary residence there.

He glanced at his watch. Half-past four. Standy would be coming along at any minute. And deep in his heart he wanted to avoid a meeting between Standy and the girl. The police are apt to be a little callous when they are hammering out the solution of a mystery. Their calling makes them so. And Gerry thought that Rosaine had had quite enough of it for one day. He had Standy's definite declaration that he was not going to arrest her. Perhaps he might yet be able to manage it.

He swung off the gate and went up the curving path. As he rounded the last bend he came into full view of the door. There was a square of white on it, standing out in sharp contrast to the dark paint. He went up closer; it was an envelope stuck on the door by the gummed edge. The address, in a neat feminine hand, was "G. Windermaine, Esq. To be called for."

He read the note it contained: –

"Dear Mr Windermaine,

"This is the only excuse I have to offer for breaking a promise. You must realise that it is quite impossible for me to see you now. So much has happened since yesterday; enough to alter the course of a life or two. Somehow it doesn't seem quite fair, the way things workout; twenty-four hours change the sunshine to darkness – and *someone* has to pay for other people's happiness.

"I am writing this knowing that you will be waiting for me at the wicket gate, in spite of my warnings of this morning. I am so much in earnest about it that I am going away, too. Perhaps now you will also go. Believe me, you are in very grave danger, so grave that I cannot emphasise it enough. Won't you please do as I ask?

"With every wish for your happiness, and a very precious memory of our first and last meeting at the wicket gate,

"Rosaine."

Windermaine squeezed the letter to a ball and thrust it into his pocket. For a minute he didn't quite know where he stood. The mists of the moor seemed to be getting into his head. It wasn't easy to think clearly when things persisted in going dead wrong at every turn. He seemed to be running his innocent head into every inadvertence that could possibly arise. And he knew that he had made a hopeless mess of things. At Deepvale there was a disastrous situation waiting for his return. At Rose Cottage there was the blank wall of a complete impasse. And so far as he could see there was not a single ray of light on the whole bleak skyline.

All he knew was that he didn't want to meet Standy just then. Standy had spent too long in the shallows. All his life he had been rubbing shoulders with the lower orders of humanity, and he had absorbed something of their harsher outlook on life. He was blunted – and not a little cynical – where the sweeter intimacies of life were concerned. He would have offered a few pithy inches of advice pitched in a caustic, acidulated key. And Gerry was in no mood to be told he had made a fool of himself.

Heartsmeet petered out at the far end into the broad face of the downs. There was no definite end to it; it just seemed to lose itself in a broken tumble of underbush, gorse, and thin-poled fir trees. It was a part of the moors he had not yet visited, and he struck out that way, whistling shrilly for his dog.

Harrigan had told him of a fine pond up there, a forty-acre swelling of a small river. The river itself was so insignificant that it dried away to a mere trickle in summer, but the pond remained – a lurking ground for a particularly hungry-jawed family of pike.

The gardener, who fished there frequently on his off days, had recommended it for a good afternoon's sport, and had given him directions for finding the place where he kept his rods and baits. The place was secluded, right away in among the higher downs, a sort of natural, untapped reservoir in the mists and the solitudes.

He could hardly have invented a better spot for an afternoon's quiet thinking. Sitting up there, with a line out over the waters, he could probably get down to some sort of a solution to the tangle that had grown up around him.

One thing was obvious, and that was that a course of action – the right one – would have to be decided on before he could possibly go back and face Valerie at Deepvale. As it was, he was floundering up to his neck in good intentions, without the faintest notion of how best to put them into effect.

He plodded on manfully, the only moving dot of life in the whole broken expanse of desolation. By five o'clock he had breasted the top of the first row of downs. The pond, or the Black Deep, as it was called locally, was away over in the first dip of the next hill, about a mile off.

He turned and looked back into the valley. Rose Cottage was visible from there, a dainty little doll's-house, nested sweetly in its bower of trees. But there was no Standy waiting at the door. Heartsmeet, the whole length of it, was deserted.

The light was still good; up there in the smokeless air, in spite of the rain mist, the light would be good for three hours yet. It was still more than strong enough to have seen Standy had he been there. But there was no sign of him. Only the emptiness, the forlorn look of a place deserted, that had depressed him unaccountably when he was sitting on the gate.

Puzzled, he pushed on over the brow of the hill. Standy was such a definite, deliberate sort of chap that he was a bit worried over it. The detective, he knew, was more than keen to have a long talk with the girl. There would not be much mercy about him either, until he had found out what he wanted. His absence at Rose Cottage might have meant that he had already got on the track of her – Standy had a way of finding things out about two hours ahead of the clock. Gerry prayed that her hiding-place had not been found already. She was having a bad enough time without having Scotland Yard hounding her about.

His line of thought was interrupted by the sight of a sturdy, hurrying figure coming down the opposite hill. He was almost running, and when he caught sight of Windermaine he began waving his arms excitedly and shouting to him at the top of his voice. Gerry couldn't hear a word he was saying, but it was obvious that the man was extraordinarily agitated. Finally he began to run, flying down the slopes as fast as his legs could carry him.

Something of his excitement communicated itself to Gerry and he found himself increasing his own pace. Then he broke unto a jog-trot, which got quicker and quicker until finally he was galloping down to meet him in a long steady run, that covered the ground at a rare pace.

For he suddenly realised the identity of the man coming down the hill. It was Pymm, the head gardener at Deepvale Manor, his friend of the fishing pool. And Gerry knew from experience that he was not normally an excitable individual. On the contrary, he was a typical Devon downsman, as stolid and imperturbable as the hills that hemmed him round.

Gerry had taken a quick and instinctive liking to the man; his calm, phlegmatic way of going about his business was so eminently confident and assuring; he knew his job inside out, and he conveyed the impression of absolute dependability.

To see him flying down the hill waving his arms and bawling hoarsely, was so totally unlike him that Gerry was quite prepared to discover that something prodigious had happened. When the man finally babbled out his story Gerry thought the man must have suddenly taken leave of his senses. For the story he told was unbelievable, incredible.

He pulled himself up, dishevelled, panting, a wild look of fright in his eyes. He was sickly white round the mouth, and he was trembling. It was some time before he could speak; he just stood staring at Windermaine, his chest going up and down like a pair of bellows, jerking his scared face round every now and then to glance back at the crest of the hill.

"What's wrong, Pymm?" asked Windermaine.

"The Deep, sir?" gasped the gardener. "The Black Deep – it's gone!"

"Gone? What do you mean?"

"It – it's gone! It isn't there! There's no Black Deep left – only the hole where it used to be!"

Gerry looked at him intently. The man was sober enough; he remembered that Harrigan had mentioned that he was a rabid teetotaller. And he seemed perfectly sane. Except for his undoubted fright he was a normal human being, altogether too steady to be suffering from hallucinations.

"I'm afraid I don't quite understand you," said Windermaine. "Get a grip on yourself, man – a pool *can't* vanish — "

"But it has, sir – it has!" declared the gardener. "The whole forty acres of it; there isn't a drop of water in it. Not a drop. It's bone dry. And after that deluge we had during the night. There are rows and rows of border plants washed right out of the ground down in the Manor, sir – but up there that pool is as dry as the Sahara. And it's hot, sir, hot! You can see the heat rising from it. It stinks. There's weeds there a foot thick, and they're cooking! I knew it was happening, sir, I knew something awful was going on up at the Black Deep. I saw it this morning when I was out doing the hot-houses. Six in the morning it was, with the light hardly started in the sky, and — "

Gerry took him firmly by the arm and led him back the way he had come.

"Come on, Pymm, don't be a fool," he snapped. "What are you running away for? You'll be going off into a blind panic if you don't pull yourself up. Now, steady down a bit. That's better. There's nothing to — "

"But you can't understand, sir," broke in the gardener, nervously. "You haven't seen it – you don't understand what's happened. I know the run of these hills like I know my own gardens – and there's nowhere that water could have gone. That lake was near half a mile across in parts and I've fished it with a hundred feet of line down over the side of a punt. A hundred feet of it, sir. That means thousands and thousands of tons of water; all down in the hollow. And it's gone! It couldn't have flowed out, unless it climbed over the top of the downs."

Gerry held him and kept on walking.

"All right, then," he said, pacifyingly. "We will take it for granted that the Black Deep has dried up in a night. That's no excuse for hysterics. I'll come back there with you and we will see if we can't find some explanation for it. Miracles don't happen these days, Pymm."

"Don't they?" retorted the gardener, doggedly, and the accents of fear were running loose in his voice again. "I might tell you, sir, I've seen more miracles happening down here the last few months than ever I've read about in the Bible. Evil miracles, too. Things that mean death for those that see them. And I want to get out of the place. It's haunted by devils. That mad scientist is out at his games again. He's in league with the Evil One himself. If you'd seen what I've seen going on here you'd know whether miracles happen or not. And I saw that one happening myself."

"*You* did?"

"Yes, sir, I did. There's no use shutting your eyes to facts. When I was coming up out of the furnace hole of the hot-houses this morning I turned and looked up on that hill. I do it most mornings, for a weather sign. But this morning I couldn't help looking up. There was a glow over the hill, right over the whole lot of it, sir. Not the green and blue flicker you see sometimes over there by the Pendine Caves, but a deep red glimmer, red as blood!

"When the light grew stronger I could see a great cloud. It was rising, rising all the time like a thick fog. It was raining solid, a steady downpour without a breath of wind in the air, and the steam was going up like a huge column to the sky. I'd reckon it was half a mile high, sir, and I knew there was something dreadful happening up here. We're bewitched, sir, that's what we are. And there's nothing but horror waiting for us."

Windermaine stopped in his tracks.

"Pymm," he said, coldly, "you're a fool. And you're in no state to come back to the Black Deep. I believe if a grouse rose under your feet right now you'd begin screaming. Go back. Go back to Deepvale and ask to see Mr Standy, the gentleman who arrived this morning. Tell him I'm up here, up at the Black Deep, and that something has happened. Tell him I want him urgently – that nothing else matters. You understand?"

Pymm nodded with unabashed relief. Nothing was plainer than that he literally dreaded the thought of going back to the Black Deep.

"Yes, sir, yes, I'll tell him," he said, and hurried off before Gerry could get a chance to change his mind.

Windermaine watched him go, then turned and pushed rapidly on to the Black Deep. And, unknown to him and unseen, dogging along like a black shadow of doom a hundred yards behind him, crawled the stealthy figure of Carlo Damian.

10

THE TRAIL OF MYSTERY

Windermaine cut across the side of the hill and struck the footpath, a mere dark rut that crawled over the downs from the village. The going was easier there. It was free, at least, from the unending clutter of gorse and brush and heather tufts that scarred the rest of the downs.

Pymm had exaggerated, of course. He knew that before he breasted the brow of the hill. The true West Countryman is only one degree less superstitious than the Irish. His beliefs are steeped in folklore, permeated with a heritage of the old legends of the sea. The gardener had seen things that were not there.

Probably a chasm had opened in the bed of the Black Deep and some of its water had sunk away. Such occurrences were not unknown. A sudden subsidence of the lake bed, made possible by a flaw in the hill strata, would account for a good deal of water. It would have lowered the level of the Deep by several feet, and until the river filled it up it would naturally present a somewhat extraordinary aspect.

Windermaine was quite sure in his own mind that something of the sort had happened: that, if the waters of Black Deep *had* appreciably lost volume, there was a perfectly logical explanation for it. He believed that, in spite of his knowledge of the other amazing things that had happened in the locality. He believed in spite of the streak of death, the mangled swan, the Pendine Lights, as the country folk had come to call them; in spite of the mutilated hare and the weird demonstration of the disintegrating rays in Deepvale Manor.

For, in comparison with Pymm's assertion, all the rest were very small meat. They were equally mysterious, of course, and, so far as his own scientific knowledge went, they were all equally impossible of explanation.

A mad genius, experimenting with a hitherto undiscovered principle, might quite conceivably be able to knock over a hare on the run, or bring a great swan down in a fearfully broken condition.

With a stretch of imagination he might even abolish life from the soil of a given area – certain chemicals will render the most perfect arable land sterile for years. But, clever though they were, they were feats that paled into insignificance in comparison with the total elimination of forty acres of water. That was something that soared right up beyond the bounds of the possible. It simply could not be done.

No, it was just that Pymm had allowed the happenings of the past few months to play on his mind. Native superstition had done the rest. He had been talking with his cronies, and, true to their type, the old villagers had succeeded in seeing things that never existed in any world of hard facts. Fear had been born. He and the rest of the folk around were ready to believe anything.

Windermaine strode on for another hundred yards and then he topped the summit of the hill.

Sheer in his tracks he stopped, pulled up as short as though he had run into a brick wall. He stood in absolute amazement, unable to move, unable to act or to think or to understand, unable to do anything more than stand there and stare at the most astonishing spectacle he had ever seen in his life.

For in that sudden, amazing moment it was borne upon him that Pymm had not exaggerated by so much as a single word. Black Deep had vanished! It was gone – gone as clearly as though a mammoth sponge had been lowered from the sky and mopped up every drop of water out of it.

Where once had been a wide sweep of clear water, half a mile across, wide enough to sail a small boat on, deep enough to fish with a hundred-foot leadline without fouling the bottom, was now a vast pit that seemed to sink down into the earth like a gigantic brown quarry.

That was the first thing that struck him when the phenomenon burst upon his bewildered eyes – its complete brownness: a great brown gulf in a surrounding sea of green hills.

The lake weed that plastered the sides was as brown as the earth itself. At the bottom the weed and the reeds and the garbage of centuries lay caked in a thick layer. *And it was dry*! Even at the very bottom, where the dregs of the vanished water might have been expected to collect and drain, the deposit seemed to have dried solid.

On the top of it the bodies of hundreds of fish gleamed a dull white. The fresh, living phosphorescence had long since died from their scales. They lay torpid, dead, dull. As in all pike-ridden waters, pike predominated almost to the exclusion of all else. A few roach and bream and an occasional perch or two lay pathetically on the hard crust, but that was all.

Windermaine began trying to collect his stampeding thoughts. The thing was so hopelessly inconceivable and yet so blatantly an accomplished fact that he had been knocked right off his mental balance.

One thing was certain. Those fish had died in the water. They were dead long before the last of the water had vanished from Black Deep. As in the case of the streak of death, the water itself had been killed; the life essence was gone from it before the water itself began to disappear.

At that point he saw the great outstanding similarity between the two phenomena. The death streak was also bone dry, as dry as the withered-up bed of the lake. He remembered that there was such an absolute absence of moisture in that line of disintegration that he had been able to stick his foot far down into the soft powder that had once been wet soil.

The thing fascinated him to such an extent that he was almost surprised to find that he was walking down towards the lip of the brown bed. And walking very gingerly, too. He was stepping as touchily as though he expected to put his foot down on a keg of dynamite at every step. He paused in puzzled uncertainty at the edge.

Pymm had been right, too, about the heat waves. The place was as hot as the side of a volcano. For a moment he half hoped the explanation might be tracked down to a sudden emanation of volcanic heat from somewhere down in the foundations of the hills. And in the same breath he knew it was not possible. Not a single trace of a volcanic element had ever been located in the Devon downs: besides, the most terrible heat ever generated could not have evaporated that vast body of water in a single night.

He knew that Black Deep had been normal the previous day because Pymm had told him he had gone up after tea and laid out a lot of eel lines. And so experienced a downsman as the gardener would assuredly have noticed if anything unusual was happening at the pool.

He stepped out on to the edge of the dead lake. A cloud of choking, stenchant dust rose all around him and got into his lungs. It made him sneeze violently. It was pungent as snuff and infinitely finer than the finest ground chalk.

Wherever he put his feet the weeds and the litter fell to powder under his boots. As in the death streak, the living things had been atomised; there was not a spark of vitality left in the whole great expanse of it.

About a dozen boats, moored round the lake edge, still lay where they rested when the water disappeared. They lay quite still, having apparently settled very gently as the water sank. Except for the remains of an old derelict, sunk many years ago which was stuck far into the mud with its shattered timbers pointing pathetically skyward, they were all resting on an even keel.

There was one, a neat little motor-boat that belonged to the Manor, about a hundred yards away to the right. Gerry went round to it and inspected it. It looked all right; it seemed all right – until he touched it. And then he found he could poke his finger clean through it with no more effort than one needs to put a finger through a bubble.

He touched the gear lever and it came away in his hand like a piece of dried pith. Hammered steel, with no more strength in it than a rope of sand! The nickel grip was still in his hand – he squeezed it and it fell to a grey silvery powder, so fine that he blew the whole lot of it off his palm with a single breath.

He turned to go up and wait for Standy. This was a matter that required more than his own powers of deduction to think out. Two heads, and considerably more than two heads, would be wanted to get at the meaning of this new demonstration of scientific mania. So far as he was concerned, he admitted himself nonplussed. He hadn't even a thin end of a wedge he could drive in anywhere. He was simply groping through a blind fog that had neither beginning, middle nor end.

Also, he was worried. The violent death of Sir Robert Harrigan would have an immediate reaction in London. Newspaper men would be out on the trail. The title would draw them. A dozen nonentities might be waylaid and fatally injured without them taking much notice of it. But a landed gentleman with a title! The Press would smell the story behind the story. Already he could visualise the headline: "Baronet Found Mortally

Wounded Outside His Own Mansion." Special investigators would come down in shoals.

And none knew better than Gerry that a Press inquiry would precipitate a crisis. He consoled himself with the doubtful reflection that perhaps Standy could exert sufficient influence to obviate the necessity for holding an inquest. If he could persuade headquarters that it really was a matter of vital expediency, the hue and cry might be stalled off for a little while. Though how on earth headquarters could disguise the fact that a forty-acre lake had mysteriously disappeared off the face of the earth he hadn't the faintest idea.

Still, that was up to Standy. His own task, as he saw it, was to get over towards the Pendine Caves as soon as night fell and to track down those eerie lights to their source. Having done that they would be in a fair way to finding the full elucidation of the mystery.

He got to the top of the hill and looked back into the valley. There were a good many hummocks between him and the little scattering of cottages that formed the village of Deepvale. From where he stood there was not a sign of a human habitation in view. And certainly no human being. Standy, he knew – even if Pymm found him at once – would take something over an hour to get there.

He sat down on a great boulder to wait, gazing into the mighty cavity that had once held the waters of Black Deep, striving to wrest some inkling of its secret from the yawning depths. After a while he pulled out his pipe, pressed a wad of tobacco into it, and lit up.

He had been sitting there for about ten minutes, concentrating on the giant puzzle staring up at him from the dip, when he became conscious of a secondary influence creeping into his brain, slowly but with steady persistence.

The first he really knew of it was that he was becoming vaguely uneasy, unable to pin his mind to the problem written out for him across half the landscape. It was not that he was experiencing a sharp revulsion of feeling, a sudden rush of fear through his veins, or that he felt himself giving way to the strain of the high nerve tension he had been enduring throughout a whole week of scarifying incidents.

It was something far more subtle than that. He felt uncomfortable, restless, as though his inner self was trying to revolt against hidden forces that were slowly closing in on him.

It was – yes, he recognised it after a moment or two. It was the tiny voice of the subtlest instinct of all, the unsettling, unendurable conviction that unseen eyes are watching, the warning knowledge that you are not alone. It was becoming more and more intense with every moment that passed.

There are limits to every individual's ability to withstand that. And Gerry's nerves were already strained like overstressed metal. He suddenly sprang to his feet and whirled round. And as he did so he recoiled with the shock of the apparition that confronted him. Carlo Damian was standing there, less than two yards behind him, glaring down at him with a malevolence that was positively inhuman.

The black eyes were glowing like red-hot marbles; and there was a bitterness, a hatred in them that transcended anything Windermaine had ever seen in his life. It was sheer, insane ferocity crystallised into the pupils of two eyeballs.

The brows above them were matted and bushy. There was an odd quality of shagginess about them that imparted to his high dome of a forehead something of the appearance of a wild steer. But that was all the hair there was on the parchment face. The rest of the tight-drawn skin was hairless.

The great black hat pulled far down over his head bent the thin ears and gave him an indescribably satanic look. And the skull above the ears was hairless, too. It was yellowy-white, and smooth as old ivory. Long, claw-like hands protruded from slits in the heavy ulster. They hung down limply from the wrists, like the claws of some gigantic bat.

He made no sound and evinced not the slightest attempt at movement, though his whole attitude, in some electric way, seemed to declare its instant readiness to leap to the attack, or to withstand the full force of Windermaine's onslaught without giving way an inch.

It was dynamic. He looked like an unbreakable rock, a rock on which the storms of centuries had been breaking, leaving him still unbroken, still with his sombre head turned to the storm.

11

THE WORLD-DESTROYER

Gerry's hand went to his hip-pocket. When it came back his Colt was locked in his fingers. Damian did not deign to look at it. His eyes never left Windermaine's face. He just stood there like a gaunt black spectre.

It was plain for all the world to see that the man was a dangerous lunatic. No highly-skilled eye, trained to the oddities and horrors of lunacy, was required to see that the great brain inside that massive head was running loose, out of all control, like an express rushing along the metals without a hand at the controls. His insanity was the one ponderable thing about him.

Very quietly Gerry pulled back the trigger of his gun. A bullet would be the only thing that could save him in a fight with a great bull of a man like that. The click of the half-cock sounded loud on the breathless silence. Still Damian did not condescend to notice it. There was such a withering, motionless aloofness about him that his madness emerged even in his immobility.

Windermaine felt himself slipping under the spell of those unwinking eyes. If only the man would rush at him or make some movement to attack it would not have been so bad. He himself could have leapt into action, too. But that dread-full motionless stare was demoralising.

He had the gun, anyway. He had the upper hand to that extent. But beyond that point he was helpless. He couldn't very well shoot a man who just stood stock-still and regarded him with a Mephistophelean glare. Neither could he hold him up till Standy arrived. For one thing, Standy had no warrant for his arrest, and for another, there was not a scrap of direct evidence against him.

But Windermaine felt the yelling, imperative urge for action. The silent mesmerism of Damian's eyes was pulling at his nerves. He held the gun out full and square in a line with Damian's chest.

"What do you want, Carlo Damian?" he asked.

"I want you."

The answer came quiet and unhurried, as though the speaker took it for granted that Windermaine only asked the question out of pure absent-mindedness, knowing the answer as well as he did himself. It was almost as though he spoke aimlessly. The voice bore the hall-mark of high culture; it was polished, the voice of a perfectly-educated intellect.

To the younger man's heartfelt relief the madman looked away from him. He gazed down into the giant pit. His absolute indifference to that gleaming Colt was monumental. He simply ignored it. So far as was apparent, such an instrument as a death-dealing revolver had no material existence. He walked slowly to the edge of the dip.

"Yes, I want you," he repeated softly to himself, still staring into the void below. The great yellow brow puckered to a deep frown. "Thirty-three minutes," he muttered. "Thirty-three minutes, with a single wire! Wonderful! But I *knew* it. I knew it before I built the first machine. And that is where I rise greater than the others; that is where I stand immeasurably above the experimenters. Thirty-three minutes – and the Black Deep has reverted to its original electrons. And with a single wire. That is proof! The world is mine to destroy!"

He raised his massive head and his eyes ranged out to the great distances beyond the hills, to the far horizons with the swinging miles of heathered downs between. He lifted his bony hands to them, his arms raised outwards like some high priest of the Black Mass intoning a last benediction over the body of the sacrifice.

"Doomed!" he mumbled. "Doomed with all its wickedness and its sin. But a few days more and all will be as the dust of Black Deep. Dust – and the atoms of dust; ashes of a world that is no more."

Gerry went up behind him and nudged his arm with the gun.

"Don't you think you had better turn round and go home?" he said.

"No. I am not going home. I have no home," the madman replied, half-mechanically. "And I have much to do – much before the night falls. Ah! – but in a little while I will make them such a night as never shall pass away."

He turned ponderously and faced Gerry, his face alight with a mad fanaticism that only intensified the dead lifelessness of his skin.

"You hear me?" he said, his voice crackling like dried sticks. "The end of the world is here? I am bringing it about. *I am creating finality* – I, the chosen tool of a God deserted. The world is ripe for its plunge into oblivion, ripe and over-ripe. No longer is it worthy of existence.

"There is nothing but sin in the cities of men, and the peoples of the plains are sunk in iniquity. There are crime and violence upon the face of the earth. Nations make war on nations and there is no peace. The people have denied their God. The churches are deserted: sounds of revelry and the jarring discords of pleasure mock the sanctity of the Sabbath. The Holy Days are not kept. There is no reverence in the land. The more sacred the day the faster the winepresses work.

"The Day of the Crucifixion is a sign for national indulgence: the day is turned into a raucous holiday and the night is filled with drinking.

"Millions work in the arsenals of the world, piling up the weapons of death and destruction. The war-makers ride the skies, growing richer and richer on the legions of the dead and the maimed that strew their course."

He paused and his voice rose to an ominous rumble. The muscles of his face twitched with the intensity of his fervour.

"The patience of Heaven is exhausted," he cried. "The world is no longer progressing. It is slipping back. Day by day the breakdown becomes more firmly established, day by day the speed of its retrogression accelerates. It has refused to fulfil its destiny, and its existence in the divine scheme of the universe is no longer tolerated by its Creator. The earth, alone among the planets, had denied its God and His vengeance is upon it. An aeon of forbearance has availed it nothing. It is to be destroyed, reduced to its original vapours. And I, Carlo Damian, am the chosen instrument, the vehicle of the Divine will. The very hours of the earth are numbered. In a little while the star-gazers on other worlds will see the birth of a new nebula in the heavens, the reduction of the globe to its elementary gases."

Windermaine felt his skin going stiff. The madman was in earnest. There was no getting away from the dominant purposefulness of every word he uttered. He was fanatically in earnest. And no one, knowing a little of the inexplicable phenomena that had been occurring on the moors, could doubt that he had at least succeeded in producing and harnessing forces that had hitherto only existed in the nightmare phantasies of over-imaginative filmmakers.

There was the ring of maniacal sincerity in every syllable. And the genius to do it was there! He had proved that on a score of occasions during the past few weeks. He had not deluded himself with the vehemence of his religious mania. He had the gigantic brain to carry out his intentions.

Gerry began to glance round furtively for signs of Standy. If he didn't come soon, there was only one way out. The palm of his hand where he gripped the gun had gone wet and clammy.

Damian pointed down to the shrivelled-up lake-bed.

"You see that?" he demanded. "That is my first, and only, real experiment. A try-out for the great day that is so soon to dawn. A single coil of wire did that. It did it with the power generated in my test machine, a little thing no bigger than the magneto of a motor-car. It had only been running for twenty-four hours!

"In my workshop I have generators big as a battleship's turbines. And they have been running for years! Ceaselessly, day and night, the great rotors have been droning thirty revolutions to the second, storing up vast power reserves for the day when its sudden release shall see the earth crumble into dust, dissolve and disperse its atoms into the final silence of solar space.

"A single coil of wire! Tossed into the centre of the lake. An infinitesimal fraction of power transmitted through the wire and the Black Deep is no more!

"The wise men of the world will shake their heads about it and seek an explanation in theories of sudden exertions of subterranean heat. Meaning, in so many words, that the Black Deep became hot and boiled dry between midnight and dawn!

"They will tell the world that – knowing its utter fallacy. Their brains are too puny to embrace the possibility of human agency. They could never believe that a scientist has, under the grace of the higher supervision, succeeded in isolating a force that counteracts gravity and breaks down cohesion. But that is what has been attained in the Pendine Caves. That is the end to which I was born, I, the servant of the wrath of Heaven. The nullifying of the two great infinite forces.

"In a few hours there will be no more gravitation: in a little while cohesion will cease to exist. That is what has happened to the Black Deep! The cohesion of its molecules was suspended. Its weight was reduced until the zero was passed. It became lighter than air. It rose! It became more rarefied than gas. It dispersed! The Black Deep has disappeared into the infinity whence it came. A few more circlings of the hands of the clock and the earth itself will be disintegrated – mingled with the ultimate cold of the outer stars."

He stopped and eyed the younger man feverishly. A hectic spot of colour had come into his cheeks. He regarded the stalwart specimen of vigorous young manhood with gloating satisfaction.

"But first there is a rite to be performed," he hissed. "The earth must perish with every living soul upon it. But the earth must be warned. The peoples must not die in sin. Sinners must have the last great chance to repent. There is mercy for them yet, at that great fount of forgiveness that never dries up! But the time is short and the precious minutes are flying. The warning shall go forth, and you, *you* are the one who shall blazon it to the world.

"I shall take you to the Pendine Caves and you shall see with your own eyes. I will demonstrate to you, and you shall know that I speak the truth. For two seconds you shall stand in the outer nimbus of the rays of the Disintegrator. For two seconds only. You will be burned. Your hair and your skin will be obliterated. You will feel in your own body the power and the force of the principle that is going to wreck the world. And I shall take you back through the secret ways to the light. You shall be led back to the gates of Deepvale Manor to tell your story to the world. You will be a human letter, addressed to all humanity. And you will never find your way back to the great caverns where my generators roar – for you will be blind!"

For some seconds Carlo Damian stood, his eyes upturned to the dimming skies, quivering with the frenzy of his ecstatic emotion. He was livid, his spirit sublimated to the pinnacles of rapture, his body thrilling with the contemplation of the masterstroke that was trembling on the verge of consummation.

At that moment his twisted brain had convinced itself that he was the chosen instrument of the world's destruction, a servant empowered and commanded by the Creator to put a violent end to a world that had become intolerably wicked in His eyes.

Windermaine felt a nausea sweeping over him. The lunatic's fitful indifference to his presence, his way of ignoring him altogether, as though such a possibility as escape was so remote as to be nonexistent, gave the whole thing an air of nervous unreality that was horrifying.

He felt like a fly that had already been caught and trussed up in the web, with the spider just glancing at him now and then to make sure he was still there. A figment of a horrible dream in which the sleeper is half awake but unable to get back to full consciousness.

There was a great chance opening out to Windermaine. He had already guessed that Carlo Damian had discovered secret exits and entrances to the great chain of the Pendine Caves, and that his terrible inventions were housed right away down in the bowels of the downs. Those assumptions were obvious, for the Pendine Caves had been explored several times by visiting archaeologists and antiquaries, and they had discovered nothing of a series of mammoth machines being built down there in the darkness.

Damian had probably discovered a secondary cave system, either behind or below the known series, where he could work undisturbed and experiment at his leisure. If he, Windermaine, could ever get inside those hidden caves the possibilities were infinite.

With one of those queer kinks common to all lunatics, Damian was not homicidally inclined towards his victim. He might kill him, but it would be a pure inadvertence. He might kill millions of others, maliciously, but Windermaine was required for another and far greater end.

Windermaine's niche in the scheme of things was to be almost as great as his own. The Final Herald, the last messenger to a people already doomed, the last great evangelist, coming to the world with the truth on his lips and the proofs on his body, calling on sinners to repent.

Up to that point Windermaine knew he was safe. Damian would do nothing to him till he got him in front of his whirling machines. Then would be the time to act, to fight, to kill if necessary. For then he would have seen all the great caves had to offer. He could have formed some estimate of the horror that hung over the world. And, having been taken in, there was no conceivable reason why he shouldn't find his way out again.

One thing was obvious. The secrets of those caves had got to be plumbed. He had already wrecked one machine without suffering anything worse than a fierce electric shock. Perhaps, if the gods were with him, he could damage the others enough to hold up Damian till he could get in touch with Standy again. If he could only bring that about there would be sights worth seeing on the moors. Standy would get a raiding party of stalwarts down by fast cars from the Yard.

If things became really serious there would be the thunder of dynamite fulminating over the downs. Once the authorities were alive to the state of affairs there would be no kid-glove measures for Carlo Damian. There would be no quarter, no mercy until that accumulation of horrors was smashed, overwhelmed, and stamped out.

On the other hand, if he went down with Damian quietly, of his own accord, he might never come out again. The mere pressure of a button down there might be sufficient to obliterate him; and his sacrifice would be worthless. The world would swing on to its fate, helpless, ignorant of the fearful cataclysm that was swiftly closing upon it.

Why the deuce didn't Standy come? Between them they might have been able to make some sort of a show against the great brute. It seemed hours since Pymm had gone running off, with fright adding speed to his feet.

And then he remembered the gun again. With the remembrance came the flashing inspiration of a hope. He cursed himself for not having seen it before. With that gun in his fingers he held the upper hand, no matter what the subsequent circumstances might be. Golden opportunity was opening its doors to him. A little courage, a handful of grit, and the Horror of the Moors would be dissipated for ever.

Carlo Damian might be the greatest inventor the world had ever known; he might be a pioneer along lines of investigation which left the rest of science gasping; he might be the one outstanding, unprecedented brain of that or any other age – but that did not render him proof against Colt bullets fired at point-blank range. An intellect so huge that it was grotesque could not harden his skin or make his flesh impervious to the shock of nickel. And if, under the threat of sudden death, he could hold up Damian on the end of that gun, *force* him to take him through to the Pendine Caves and explain the controlling principle of his great engines of death, he might yet succeed.

Even if something did go wrong down there, even if the madman turned murderous and made a sudden rush at him, no tribunal in the land would hold him guilty of breaking the sixth commandment. Rather would they voice the gratitude and thanks of a badly-frightened world.

"Carlo Damian – put up your hands!" he said.

Damian turned from the edge of the dip and looked at him. He was still treading the heights. He did not comprehend the high lights glittering in Windermaine's eyes, did not hear the metallic warning of animosity in the keyed-up voice.

"Are you ready?" he asked.

"Put your hands up!" The words snapped at him like catapulted pebbles.

"Come, I will take you with me." Damian began to advance, heedless of the unwavering gun, regardless of the danger. The soft polish of his voice, the note of educated culture that ran through it like a golden thread, was utterly void of fear.

"Hands up, you! Back! Stand back, I say – or I'll shoot!"

Windermaine's voice had gone on to a rabid snarl. But the great hulking figure came on. He held out his hand coaxingly, as though to take his victim by the arm.

Windermaine gave him last chance.

"Get back, Damian!" he shouted. "Get back, or I'll plug every chamber into you!"

But Damian did not stop. He came on unconcernedly. He was within six yards of the gun muzzle. And Windermaine fired. With the gun pointed in a dead true line on the lunatic's heart, he pulled the trigger. There was a flash and a crack, and the echoes crashed to life amid the silence. Damian staggered a little in his walk. Gerry actually saw the shock of the impact take effect on the great chest. It rocked him back a few inches. He swayed back again, a faint look of surprise animating his placid features.

"Get back, you madman!" yelled Gerry, and fired again. Again the echoes burst in noisy clamour round the dip. Again Damian staggered under the concussion. And the devils of anger stirred in the monstrous brain. The old malevolent glare shot back into the black deeps behind the eyes; a tremor of insensate, diabolical passion quivered on his face. He went forward, his arms thrust out and grasping for the throat.

Gerry, incredulity burning every atom of restraint out of him, gave ground. He backed away, firing madly at every step. Three –

four – five – six – seven. The remaining bullets thudded hard and dry on the towering figure, but the giant came through it all, unflinching, regardless. Windermaine saw the fingers flexing and constricting within a foot of his neck. He pulled the trigger again, wildly, sheer at the avid face, but the hammer struck sharply on the empty chamber – and then the bottom of the earth opened under his feet and, with a yell, he toppled over backwards down the long slope of the Black Deep.

He bounced once, a painful collision of his shoulder-blades flat on the steep banking; then, when he rolled to the lake edge, the roll developed into a breakneck glissade on the disintegrated weeds.

A cloud of dust marked his passage, dust that swirled up in oily volumes – and kept on rising! Up and up it went on the still air, thinning out and dispersing as it rose, till it became wispy as vapour, more rarefied than steam, and then – it was gone.

Gerry came to a slithering halt, fifty feet down the side of the lake wall. The wind was knocked out of him and he was gasping for breath. The foul dust was in his eyes, in his mouth, caking his nostrils, in his very lungs. He coughed and spluttered while fresh clouds of it rose around him as he staggered up.

He waited till it cleared, unable to see a yard ahead of him. Damian was coming down the bank for him, calling on him to wait. His great swinging strides rushed him down, gesticulating wildly, jerking his body about abruptly in his efforts to maintain his balance. Gerry marvelled at his sure-footedness even in that impossible moment. For the fall of the lake-bed, where the rays had operated, was as slippery as the side of a glacier. To stand upon it was to begin to slide, as instantly and as helplessly as though the feet were planted on a thickly-larded incline. Rubbed in the fingers, the powder was a hundred times softer and more slippery than the finest French chalk.

But Damian came down it without a single slip, his ponderous boots crushing deeply into the clotted powder. It was then that Windermaine began to feel the first flutterings of panic in his heart. There seemed to be no getting away from the brute. Bullets didn't stop him. He had loosed off a whole magazine at him at point-blank range. Every one had hit him. He had seen them hit, full and square on the chest. And he had come through it unscathed, come through it with the bovine indifference of the man who did not realise what was being done to him.

Now he was caught in a trap, with the madman bearing down upon him like a gaunt black creature from another world. He tried to run, but he slithered about like a drunken man on a slide. And the choking dust clouds swirled about him again, blinding him, maddening him. For want of something for his brain to fasten on to, he began to reload his gun, futile though he knew it to be. If seven bullets, striking at 780 pounds to the square inch, failed to stop a man, there was no logical reason for supposing that fourteen would. One clip of cartridges was no more efficacious than another; and Damian was a horror who appeared to thrive on bullets.

There began a mad chase round the side of the pit, Damian storming along in his wake with never more than a few yards between them. A dozen times Windermaine heard the deep labouring of his dust-choked lungs a few feet behind his back.

Damian was not coaxing now, not even indifferent to the thoughts of his victim. He had become a hunter, relentless, unforgiving. His every effort was concentrated with a ferocious intensity on regaining his quarry. He was amazed and angry to think that his chosen emissary to a doomed world should object to playing his part. In his tormented brain it was sacrilege. The commands of the Eternal were being heretically flouted. He was hunting his victim to save its soul. He no longer spoke, but pounded on in a grim and purposeful silence.

Time after time he reached out to grasp the stumbling body ahead. Windermaine could hear the fingers clawing together just behind his ears, could feel the hot breath on his neck. And always he eluded him by getting farther into the trap. Each time he felt the bony talons snapping at him, he swayed sideways and shot a few feet farther down the pit. He got away every time, but each time he did it he was scoring a victory that brought him nearer to defeat.

Suddenly, in a violent effort to stem a more serious side-slip, he stumbled on the knack of keeping his balance and yet making progress. He found that he had jammed his feet sideways into the powder; it had crushed into a firmer cake and given him a sound foothold. Instead of digging his toes in and straining painfully to draw himself along, he stood sideways on the slope and kicked the whole side of his foot into the crust.

It gave him added encouragement, a new strength to his aching leg muscles. In a few minutes he had drawn clear and was widening the gap with every stride. He rammed the gun back in his pocket and struggled upwards, raising his dust-filled eyes to the rim, seeking salvation on the firmer ground above.

There was no boyish-chinned, questioning face peering down over the edge, silently asking itself what the dickens was kicking up all the dust. Standy seemed to have deserted him. Oh, well, it didn't matter much now; in another couple of minutes he would be out of the trap – and it would take a trained athlete to tail him off once he got his feet on solid ground. He set his teeth and climbed on, kicking up clouds of dust behind him to fog Damian.

When he was within five yards of the top he turned and looked back, labouring to get the breath back into his lungs. Damian had stopped and was looking up at him, his brows black as a thundercloud. He had seen Gerry's ruse; it was beginning to dawn on his understanding why his groping hands had not succeeded in making contact. His lips were mouthing silently up at him and his face was fused with a look of animal hate.

12

THE WOMAN WHO WATCHED

Gerry turned and mounted the last few steps. And then the spanner hit him. Flat on the base of the skull it came, a heavy, adjustable, all-metal spanner, flung by the maddened arm of the maniac. A great white streak suddenly crashed across his brain, a streak that was shot through and through with stabs of agony and silent shellbursts of red. A blackness closed down upon him. Then even the blackness vanished. Gerry Windermaine toppled over in a gentle sprawl and lay very still.

Not until that happened did the boyish-chinned, questioning face slide out for a moment from behind a boulder and gaze inscrutably down the facing. It was gone again in a moment, just a momentary vision of a black bowler hat with a face underneath it – a face on which a little row of bristles stuck out like the clipped quills of a porcupine – bristling as though with a personal affront.

Damian climbed up to where Windermaine lay. Without much effort he pulled the inanimate body up on the firmer ground above the rim of the Black Deep, and then, with a single effortless sweep, heaved it up and across his shoulders.

Three miles away the black line of the Pendine Caves showed darkly at the base of the distant downs. The light was fast failing. Long lanes of shadow reached out across the valley and blacked in the sombre shades between the hills. And the darkest line of all, the area where the shadows were piling up thickest and heaviest, was the dark smudge that marked the entrances to the outer Pendine Caves.

Carlo Damian set off across the hill towards them, Windermaine's body hanging over his shoulder as limp as an empty sack. He paused for nothing, but swept on through bracken and brushwood alike.

No sound came from behind the boulder till the rakish figure was a quarter of a mile down the hill. Then Standy sat up.

"There, did you see that?" he demanded.

Another figure sat up beside him, a figure with a helmet surmounting a frightened, unhealthily white face. It was Tendleton, the local constable. His agitation was not caused so much by the acts of out-and-out lawlessness he had just witnessed – though they were dreadful enough in all conscience – as by the much more drastic knowledge that he, for the first time in his official career, found himself in personal contact with one of those hitherto mythological beings – a C.I.D. man from Scotland Yard.

Tendleton was awed and flustered. His wildest dreams of fame had never taken him much farther than the local village toper getting drunk twice the same day, or the succesful termination of his vendetta against the two poachers who had been raiding the Harrigan preserves for the last ten years without a break – raiding them, moreover, with their thumbs to their nose and their fingers spread. Once, certainly, he had collared a motorist without a number plate, but that was so many years ago that even he could no longer raise a circle of interest with it in the local tap-room.

Now here he was, with a pension and peace for the rest of his days almost within his grasp, being dragged into what looked like being a highly objectionable fracas with the Mad Scientist. With a man who could kill wild swans in the air by merely looking at them. And also he was being commanded by the great Standy himself, who handed out strings of orders and then expected him to rush about the country as though time really mattered. Not only was the whole matter thoroughly objectionable – sixteen stone was never intended for hustle – but it looked as though it was going to turn out a highly dangerous one, too.

Standy was writing rapidly in a notebook.

"Did you see that lot?" he demanded again.

"Yes, sir," said Tendleton, aggrievedly.

"Thank Heaven for that," muttered Standy, fervently. He tore out some of his notes and pushed the bowler hat to the back of his head. "Well, that's the kind of guy you're up against," he announced. "That's the kind of chap who will be getting his grapnels on you, one of these days, if you don't step on the gas. Know where you can find your sergeant?"

"Yes, sir," said Tendleton, with quick relief. "He'd be over in Bannicombe village by this time. He's got a long beat, he has; and just about now he'd be over—"

"Take this note to him. Tell him I want help here. Need it badly. A rescue party to raid the Pendine Caves with me. Volunteers if he can't get officers quickly. Tell him to commandeer all the candles and flashlights and torches he can lay his hands on. And chalk – d'ye get me? Chalk, to blaze the trail out of the caves. I'll use my own mark – the letter S with the tail curved away and pointing in the direction I've gone."

"Er – yes, sir – I'll tell him—"

"Noble fellow. Tell him to get them up here at the run. I'll be waiting for them. There may be the devil's own light waiting for them in those hills, but—"

He broke off. Tendleton, his nerves on edge, was pointing with pop-eyed fright at a white, misty figure that was running swiftly round the edge of the rim towards them. In the gathering dusk it was seen but dimly; and in his badly jarred state Tendleton was ready to believe it was the disintegrated spirit of the vanished Black Deep. Standy turned and stared at it.

In a few seconds they saw it was a girl. She saw them and came running towards them.

She was white-faced, frigthened almost beyond speech. Standing on the other side of the lake-bed she had seen the fight in the dip, and her eyes told of the horror that charged her soul.

"That's Valerie Harrigan, isn't it?" whispered Standy, and Tendleton nodded vigorously. Standy was astounded to see her there. "Now, how the blazes did *she* get here!" he said. "She's going to duff the whole show if she starts streaking off into hysterics." He motioned her to silence. But Valerie was too overwrought to think coherently about anything just then. She came up to them, her breast heaving spasmodically and her eyes blazing with something that was very near to indignation.

"You – you're Standy, the detective from London, aren't you?" she burst out.

Standy raised his hat an inch. "Yes, miss – not quite so loud, if you don't mind. There's a—"

"And you – you dare to stand there – with a policeman by your side – the pair of you – and see a man half-killed before your eyes. You don't attempt to raise a finger to save him. You great hulking—"

" 'Sh! Steady, Miss Harrigan, please!" cut in Standy.

But Valerie ignored his danger signals.

"You know who these two men are?" she demanded. She was almost on the point of a break-down.

"Yes – one was Carlo Damian," said Standy, quietly.

"And – and the other was Gerry!" she flung back at him. "Gerry Windermaine! For Heaven's sake, save him! Damian will kill him. Do something! You *must* save him! Bring him to me. I must see him – I must – I must—"

"Miss Harrigan," said Standy, grimly, "if you don't control yourself and talk quietly, I'll gag you! You'll have Damian coming back! Your voice carries in this air. Windermaine's all right; you can rely on that. My only hope of—"

"But you don't understand," cried Valerie, feverishly. Her eyes were very bright and she was twisting her hands about in an effort to stifle her emotion. "Pymm told me of the awful happening up here. I came up. And I saw Gerry being nearly murdered. You cowards! You let it happen! But Damian shan't kill him – he shan't!"

She turned and made a flying rush after the fast-vanishing figures in the distance, with Standy pounding along at her heels.

He caught her and forced her to a standstill. "Tendleton," he called back in a low voice, "get back to Bannicombe and find your sergeant. Quickly! Wait for nothing!"

Tendleton stood up and lumbered off.

"Now, Miss Harrigan," he said, turning to her angrily, "if you don't exercise a little restraint I'll arrest you for impeding an officer in the execution of his duty. And that's flat! I know exactly what you're feeling and, believe me, I sympathise with you sincerely. But that's no excuse for wrecking everything just when things are getting to a crisis. I know perfectly well what I'm doing – and your hysteria doesn't help me a bit. You'll either see Windermaine alive and well tomorrow morning – or you'll never see anything more on earth. You won't even live through the night. That's the size of it."

She caught earnestly at his arm.

"But – but – " she faltered "You don't know what I saw on the other side of that dip, Mr Standy—"

"What – what's that? Who else was there?"

"Rosaine! That horrible witch woman. I saw her. She was watching them fight. When Gerry began to shoot she went running off, silently, but fleet as a hare – through the bushes—"

Standy took her by the shoulders.

"Where – which way did she go?" he asked, staring straight into her eyes.

Valerie pointed towards the great black ridge.

"Over – over there!" she said, faintly. "They will kill him together. Oh, why don't you—"

Standy turned her round.

"Go home!" he said, harshly. "Get back to Deepvale and wait for me at the Manor. I will bring you news as soon as I can." He watched her stumble away through the gathering shadows.

"Gosh! Here's a lively kettle of fish," he growled. "Gerry, my boy, you're in the very deuce of a mess!"

He looked round to the dark line of the Pendine Caves, jammed his hat firmly on his head, and stole off hurriedly on the heels of Carlo Damian.

13

THE SECRET OF THE CAVES

Standy pushed along, getting over the ground quickly yet with a silence that was almost cat-like. Only the soft rustle of his clothes against the gorse, or the even softer scuff of his boots through the occasional grass patches, betrayed his flitting presence.

The stolidly striding form of Carlo Damian was dimly ahead in the distance, a moving silhouette against the blur of the gathering gloom. He forged ahead through everything, spurning the prickly scrub, oblivious of the clinging brambles.

Standy broke into a run until he had shortened the distance between them. Then he eased, and kept up a steady fifty yards' gap, dodging along in Damian's wake like a detached shadow.

Among the greying half-tones he was like a faint wraith, difficult to keep track of. One minute he was a half-suspected shadow away on the right, slipping and sliding from cover to cover; the next he was a vaguely discerned form away to the left, flickering swiftly from heather to bramble, from bramble to whin-clump. But always in the line of sudden cover.

There were not ten yards of the whole journey when Standy was not within a jump of cover, not a moment when Damian could have whipped round and found anything but a lonely, empty heath behind him.

But Damian did not look round. That was the remarkable thing about him. He seemed to have got back to his own mountainous indifference. His mind embraced but a single thought, the final accomplishment of his evil schemes. All else was subordinated to that. There was not room in his unstable brain of hostile considerations. Who would *want* to stop him, or even hinder him, in the consummation of so great a duty as had been entrusted to him? Who, knowing the source of his inspiration, would even attempt to check its due obedience?

Only one, perhaps. And he was slung across his shoulders.

As the great bulk of the caves loomed ahead Standy closed the gap. He slid along between masses of granite rock – fragments broken away from the great formations overhead – until, when Damian suddenly swung in through one of the yawning holes in the rock wall, Standy was treading on his shadow, with his boots off!

The Pendine Caves were a curiosity in the district. Geologists were at a loss to account for their presence there. The oddity about them was that they should never have been there at all. They were a distinct flaw in the earth strata, a huge formation of honeycombed granite, rearing up at the side of the downs. Granite runs in veins. Yet there was no other granite within miles of that giant mass. It was a solitary upthrow, unaccountable, inexplicable.

How far they penetrated into the hill no one knew. Metallurgists and geologists were at variance on the matter. The only points they were agreed upon were that the caves were undoubtedly there and that their existence was probably due to a subterranean convulsion right away back in the dawn of time, when the unthinkable pressures exerted by the contracting earth forced the granite fluke upward from some hidden vein miles deep below the settled crust.

It was typical of Damian that he should have plumbed the whole chain of them from end to end, discovered the hidden connecting chambers, and solved the mysteries that had baffled skilled explorers for generations. Moreover, he knew his way about the cavernous passages blindfold. Standy discovered that early on. He had been hoping that Damian would need a light. However slight it was, it would have been sufficient to have kept him on the trail. Sufficient, too, to have scrawled up his hurried S's and know that the tails pointed true.

As it was, it was mostly guesswork. The caves were shockingly rough and his feet were in dire straits long before he had penetrated the second hundred yards. For him it was a nightmare chasing of an echo through a black labyrinth of tortuous windings.

After a while the sound of a faint murmuring merged on the silence. It was elusive, soft as the rustle of tissue-paper in the impenetrable fastnesses of the caverns. At first he thought it was the hum of Damian's great machines, but after a minute he dismissed the thought. There was nothing metallic about it, nothing definite enough to have been born of humming metals.

The hunt led downhill – had been doing so almost from the first moment of entering the caves. He could feel that, even in the pitch darkness.

The murmuring grew steadily louder and louder. All at once, as they turned a sharp corner, he recognised it as the sound of rushing water – a subterranean waterfall.

Damian led him on till the noise of falling water was booming in his ears, filling the great caverns with a thunder of noise. It rose and swelled about him in a bellow of sound, growing more and more oppressive on the ear-drums with every minute that passed.

The man ahead turned sharply off and headed down through a narrow split in the rock. Standy followed, five yards behind, with the walls almost touching him as he went forward. He crawled through the opening and the deafening clamour burst upon him in full force. He knew that he was standing within inches of the falling column of water. He knew it from the sudden crescendo of noise, from the rush of cold air on his face, from the bursting spray that filled the air like fine, persistent rain.

Damian had gone on. There was not even the echo now of his great boots rinsing on the granite floor. And ahead was a death-trap of plunging waters. Standy waited for a lead. None came. He took his courage in both hands and switched on his torch. The warm glow lit up the lower part of the cavern, reflecting off the thundering water in a hundred dancing beams, flashing back from the wet walls in shimmers of yellow fire.

The water was falling solidly, black as ink in the darkness, from some mighty gash far up in the vaulted roof. He raised his torch, but its light was insufficient to dissipate the darkness. A feeble reflection shone, at about forty feet high, still on water, so that the fall must have been from a great height.

But apart from that the cavern was empty. Of Carlo Damian and Windermaine there was not a sign. All around rose the giant walls, sheer and black and wet. Not a break, not a crack showed anywhere in the high smoothness of their lines. There was not enough concealment for a rat. It was like the nave of some vast cathedral, rearing up into an enormity of blackness above, but as lonely as a mountain peak.

Standy muttered things under his breath and stared round at the circling wetness. Damian couldn't possibly have gone back up that narrow approach. There was barely room for one, let alone two. Damian was still there – somewhere.

There was only one explanation. Impossible as it was seemed, Damian must have gone on right through the waterfall.

Standy felt his way to the end of the chamber. Below him, in a boiling flux, the vortex of the fall seethed and hissed. The drop was sheer. No man could have made that descent and lived to come back out of it. The space between the fall and the break in the floor was less than two feet. And the water had a hidden outlet somewhere beneath the cave.

Standy lay out on his face along the floor, leaning out as far as he could over the drop, and thrust his arm through the sheeting fall. He found exactly what he had expected. The waterfall, though high and wide, was not of such great volume as had at first appeared in the unreflecting darkness. The wall of water was only a foot thick. Beyond it, behind the fall, was a continuation of the cave. The waterfall was nothing more than a colossal curtain, falling continuously, shielding the entrance to the other great cave series.

Standy stood up, his hair and his clothes drenched with the flying spray.

"Gerry," he muttered, "this is where Scotland Yard takes a quiet step to the rear and pretends it hasn't noticed anything. Up there, on the first floor, as one might say, is an exceedingly charming girl of the name of Valerie. You concern her – but, apparently, she doesn't concern you. Down here, in the basement, is – what? I'll lay all Devon to a blackberry on Rosaine! And in that case Detective Standy steps as daintily as a fairy. If I barge in there, Rosaine comes into all the muck and mud of the police-courts, trials, inquests, and what not. And Windermaine would just about brain me!"

He thought of it all back to that one very definite conclusion, his authority being that he had taken a quiet peep at that letter long before Windermaine had torn it off the door at Rose Cottage.

"Bob Standy," he said, gently, " 'bout turn, my son. Keep your nose out of it till they have squared their own little account. You get your chance when the boys arrive."

Very carefully he felt his way back, picking out his blaze on the rock walls, improving it as he went.

14

THE HOUR OF DOOM

Standy went slowly back to Deepvale Manor, and in his mind was a nightmare darkness and a nightmare fear. There seemed to accompany him, step by step, the ghost of Carlo Damian, Damian the madman, whose spirit was all of evil, whose twisted heart was all of stone, Damian the avenger, with his crazy, haunted eyes.

Damian, the bitter dreamer, the man of terror who had dared to league himself against the world of men! The world slept, did not even know the madman's name. London slept at this hour, or went gaily about its playtime under the city's million lights, amused itself with noise and with laughter in theatres and restaurants and places where they dance.

While he now went stumbling through the darkness, they made love and cheer and music through the careless hours. Nothing they knew of Carlo Damian. Nothing they knew of the Terror he could fling loose upon them, the Great Sleep of Destruction he willed to visit them all at a single touch of his madman's hand!

Standy heard himself gasp as the thought took him, and found that he stopped still, dead still, upon his way. It was the thought of *time*, and the thought crushed him.

When ?

When did Carlo Damian propose to unleash that avenging ray? Upon that the world's fate depended, and that dread secret was the madman's own.

Standy knew more than most of that tiny band of scientists and great statesmen who had wrested some inkling of Damian's mighty task. A dozen great names made up that council of research and of defence, and there had been no meeting Standy had not attended. Now he shrugged his shoulders and pressed on.

"The crazy devil isn't ready yet, I'm sure of it," he said, aloud. "But when does he *expect* to be ready? I wish I knew! Hullo! What's up now?"

He began to run. For he had rounded the high trees that gave him sight of Deepvale Manor, and the poor light of candles showed in every window. It was pathetic and eerie, and the flickering lights seemed to make of the great building a house of poverty and shame. He saw a door wide open, and ran still harder for it, crying out as he ran.

It was a woman who answered the cry. She showed in the doorway, uncertain, unreal, a trembling phantom of a woman from whom, for this stricken hour, her usual pride and the courage of her race had been swept clean away.

"Miss Harrigan!"

She remained where she was, still a phantom, still shaking, still silent.

"Miss Harrigan," the man called, sharply. "What's the matter? Get back to the house if you're ill; you've no right to be out-of-doors. Do you hear me?"

"The house," the girl repeated, tonelessly. And she shivered. "Back there? I won't go back. I'm afraid. I want you to leave me alone, that's all. It's not a house any more – it's a tomb, or it will be. That's why I lit all the candles – one for every window. Do you think father" – her voice broke – "will be the only one to die?"

Standy took her by the arm. She was facing a break-down, and he knew it. He spoke sharply.

"This is nonsense. I'll get one of the maids. It's bed for you, my girl."

He stepped inside the house, and called loudly, "Hawkins! Quick, man!"

There was no answer. Three times he called the butler's name, and no answer came. Standy stepped about the great hall, opened a door and banged it to gain, rapped noisily with his heavy stick upon the top of an old dower chest. One of the candles Valerie had set near the entrance went out mournfully, another followed – and even Standy discovered himself repressing a touch of fear. It angered him. The scorn on the face of the silent woman near him lit his temper. He turned to her.

"What's the matter with this house?" he demanded. "Is everybody asleep, confound them?"

She shook her head. Her sad eyes pitied him, and, resentfully, he knew that she saw him as a great blundering child. She spoke to him rather as a woman speaks to a child.

"You're stupid, I'm afraid, Mr. Standy. It's you who are asleep. Call them again – if you like. You won't get any answer – unless my dead father speaks—"

"Won't I?" Standy retorted. "I'll wake somebody up, and have you being looked after properly in the next three minutes."

Again he called the names of the servants he knew. But nothing happened. His voice, usually so robust and charged with command, seemed to fail. Standy's command and authority died. He turned to the girl with a blank and humble face, and in his voice a humility he had never known till that moment.

"I'm sorry, Miss Harrigan. I'll ask you to forgive me. It hasn't been such an easy job for me – you know that. What *has* happened?"

"There's no living soul in Deepvale Manor except you and me," she answered. "It happened quite suddenly – they were scared out of their lives. Even Hawkins, who swore he would stand by me. I tried to persuade them, but it was no use. They've all gone. They're all frightened out of their lives."

"Bolted, eh?" muttered Standy, grimly. "Well, you're not that sort, thank Heaven!"

She took courage. She found the man's hand suddenly in hers.

Standy went on, quickly: "I'm not so sure it isn't a good thing they've gone. People with the coward mind get in the way; they haven't any grip. We shan't have to think about them. We can do things ourselves in the way we want them done."

Valerie nodded. "Well, what are you going to do? I'll do anything, Mr. Standy – except stay in this house of the dead. Don't look at me like that – I'm all right now. I'm not afraid of anything."

Standy commended her with a whisper. "Good girl! Well, I'm sure you needn't worry about Gerry. I know the way that madman's mind works. I—"

"Mr. Standy, don't try to deceive me. Are you sure of that?"

"I'm positive. I'll tell you why. Damian's got Gerry safe in the Pendine Caves, and thinks he can do what he likes with the lad. That crazy type wants an audience above all things – remember Damian has worked at his fiendish plans absolutely alone for years. Now that he has Gerry helpless, he'll be bursting to show him all the wonders of the machine in the caves. He'll gibe at Gerry Windermaine. He'll threaten him all the time. But he'll not rest till he has shown him everything, every appalling detail of his diabolical inventions. He'll torment Gerry with suspense. I'm right, Miss Harrigan – you've got to believe me. We've got to wait for a bit, hard as it is. We've got to mark time."

Very carefully Standy watched her, for there was no such certainty in his own heart. But just now the only thing to do was to make as sure as a man could that Valerie was easy in her mind about Gerry – was not alarmed, at any rate, for him. And Standy's bluff succeeded. The girl nodded, and then, suddenly, she seemed to take charge.

"I'll do what you tell me, and I'll think no more of Gerry," she declared. "But we haven't got to wait, Mr Standy – you're wrong there. There's no time for standing still, and you ought to know it. Goodbye, Mr Standy!"

Again her voice was scornful. She darted away from him. Only for a second or two did Standy pause and wonder. Then he was at her side.

What's in your mind?"

"I'm going to Rose Cottage, of course," she said. "Rosaine's there, I suppose – and isn't she our only chance of getting safely into the caves to fight Damian? If you can't frighten that witch-woman into helping us, perhaps I can!"

Standy only grunted, but he knew that, in a way, Valerie was right. The woman at his side, from whom an urgent fire of hate and passion had driven out all fear, went with the long strides of a man. It was sometimes difficult for him to keep up. In a little while they could see a light in Rose Cottage. Valerie Harrigan was a woman sure of her errand; she walked more quickly still. She knocked at the door of the cottage. There was no reply. Standy heard her murmur of impatience. She knocked again, and Rosaine opened the cottage door,

Valerie eyed her like an enemy. Rosaine's confused inquiry as to their business angered her. Rosaine made an attempt to close the door, and the other girl pushed by her into the cottage. The detective followed.

"Shut that door, Mr. Standy," Valerie ordered. She turned to the other woman. "Listen to me. How long will it take you to show us the way – the safe way – into the Pendine Caves?"

Rosaine looked at her questioner and seemed to smile. But there was no hatred in her look. There was nothing of anger or contempt. She simply shook her head.

"Are you not going to answer?" Valerie demanded, and there was a little pause.

"I have answered," she said. "And I want to warn you. Do not stay in this cottage, if you please, a moment longer than you can help. You will be safer out there on the moor. There is nothing for you here – nothing. Nothing but danger. This tiny cottage is a place of darkness and of fear. Please go away."

There was a longer silence now. Valerie's glance measured her rival. The face of Rosaine was expressionless and white. Standy, watching them both, forgot his curiosity over Rosaine's odd words in a new moment of wonder at her beauty. Valerie leaned a little forward. "They call you the witch-woman in this parts of the world," she said. "They are ignorant and stupid people, of course, but I wish you were a witch – and that the old laws against witches still held. It is because of you – only because of you – that Gerry Windermaine is now lying helpless in the Pendine Caves – helpless with that brute Carlo Damian."

"Wait!" cried Rosaine, anxious entreaty in her voice. "Wait! I—"

But Valerie took no notice.

"I do not know what your relationship with Damian is, and I don't care. I'm thinking of Gerry Windermaine, and of nobody else. I want you to take me in safety to Carlo Damian, so that I can talk with him. I tell you you must do this for me, and you must do it now. Heavens, girl! how can you refuse?"

"I do not refuse," Rosaine assured her, quietly. "I only tell you that it is impossible. Do you think that Damian has lived and worked in the caves all this time without taking steps to deal in his own way with unwelcome visitors? Mr Standy was wise to come back. You would not step one foot beyond the opening to the caves and remain alive for a minute!"

"I don't believe you," retorted Valerie, and Rosaine answered her rather sadly.

"It is true," she declared. "There are many things you don't understand. It is useless for you to get angry. Stay in this cottage if you like. I am going."

She moved towards the door, so quietly and with such a look in her eyes that she seemed like a woman of a dream. Valerie watched her with a sort of fascination, conscious of a feeling of admiration. Then the spell the witch-woman appeared to have cast upon them broke. Valerie moved very swiftly and placed her back against the door.

"I think not," she said, in a dangerous voice. "We're not fools. It's not going to be so easy as that for you, Rosaine."

The other woman lifted her tired eyes. "I have work to do on the moor," she said, gently. "Let me go. You can follow me if you like – and if you dare!"

"There will be no need for that," retorted Valerie, "because you are going to stay here. Do you understand? *Here*! You are my prisoner, Rosaine. You are still pretending you do not understand? I will be quite plain. You are my prisoner so long as Gerry Windermaine is Carlo Damian's prisoner. When Gerry comes back to me safe and sound, I will let you go – but not till then. Sit down!"

Standy murmured something, whether a word of approval or of protest Valerie neither knew nor cared. She moved slowly forward, almost pressing Rosaine back with her body.

Standy saw Rosaine seated against her will by the great open fireplace, saw Valerie still stooping over her. He was aware of a second's wondering expectation that Valerie would actually strike the other woman.

Suddenly a car skidded with atrocious violence in the lane outside, and the noice of its tortured brakes made a tragic screaming that tore at Standy's nerves. Quickly as he moved, there were others more quick than he. Their urgent knocking crashed thunderously on the cottage door. Standy pulled the door open and stood still in astonishment, before he uttered the visitor's name.

"Sir Guy! What on earth—"

Sir Guy Crosland, the head of the Institute of Research that had been founded a year before by the Government for purposes of Imperial Defence, stepped over the threshold.

"I'm glad to find you here, Standy," he said. "We drew Deepvale Manor first – and I was afraid. I've got the secretary of our Defence Committee with me. And I'll not dare to go back – unless something happens here that leaves Damian stark and cold. When I heard from you, Standy, how far Damian had gone with his devilish inventions, I knew at once that there was no time to lose. And since then—"

Standy interrupted. "Another fortnight!" he said.

Sir Guy looked at him queerly.

"That's where you're wrong, Standy," he said, in a voice that cracked with anxiety and strain. "Damian is ready to strike now. Early this evening a messenger from Damian delivered an ultimatum. He can reach London with this ray of his – and I know he's right. Carlo Damian promises to destroy London at five o'clock tomorrow! And he means it – to the very second!"

The three men confronted Rosaine, still in the chair to which Valerie Harrigan had driven her.

One by one, Sir Guy Crosland, Charles Carpenter, secretary of the Defence Committee, and Standy flung questions at her that were like the lashings of a whip.

They had questioned her for the last twenty minutes. They had striven to obtain from her something at least of the secrets of Damian's machines. They had demanded dates of her – when had Carlo Damian first come to this part of the world, where and from whom had he obtained his marvellous knowledge of his special sciences and their applications, what colleagues had he possessed in the working out of his knowledge, and where were they to be found now?

Rosaine had never hesitated to answer them. And her answers had made them wiser, but had not lessened their anxiety, had not decreased by an atom the fear that held their souls captive. At the finish, it was Standy who crystallised the thoughts and hopes of them all in one last hopeless question.

"How can we get hold of Damian, Rosaine? Tell us that."

He had expected nothing but an evasion or a direct lie. The girl's answer electrified him. He saw her glance at the tall clock; then she said:

"He will be here in ten minutes."

"What?" cried Standy. "Are you sure?"

"Certain."

She rose. Her lithe young body looked strangely weary as she moved across the room. The three men and Valerie watched her with a kind of absorption as she took from a shelf a small black cardboard box. Standy saw a much larger box near it, and knew instinctively what both boxes contained.

"Morphia, eh?" he murmured. "That's one thing I didn't know about Carlo Damian!"

"He has taken it for years," Rosaine told him. "This box of tablets came here only this morning, and he has forgotten them. That is why I knew he would be back from the caves. It is his exact time for an injection."

For all the interest she betrayed in the others, they might not have been there at all. Rosaine opened the larger box, took out a hypodermic syringe, and laid it aside. She moved a small kettle over the fire. The water in it was already hot, and in a minute she poured a little of it into a squat glass. Into the glass she dropped three of the morphia tablets.

"Three, eh!" muttered Standy, astounded, for he had seen the marked strength of the tablets. "No wonder the man's crazy."

"He said," Rosaine told him, "that this would be the last box of tablets he would ever want."

Sir Guy made a gesture of hopelessness. It seemed a trifling piece of news, but its implication was tremendous and sinister. Damian had reached the end of his task; that was what he had meant, nothing less. No more would he require the stay and urge of morphia. The thing was done. Sir Guy found himself muttering under his breath. "Five o'clock tomorrow—"

"Hush!" warned Rosaine, and raised her hand slightly. They heard the uneven steps of a man who approached the cottage. Rosaine moved towards the door, and in that second Standy had his inspiration, and was very quick to act upon it. Only Sir Guy saw his purpose, and he smiled.

Standy took three more of the tablets from the little black box, took them with untrembling fingers, and dropped them into the glass of hot water. A second more and he was back in his own place. If Carlo Damian, drug-fiend as he was, took that full dose, Standy's work was finished – goodbye to Carlo Damian and to the menace that overhung the world!

Now Damian stood in the doorway and surveyed them all. Dark and sure and malevolent, he laughed at them with his terrible eyes and his purring voice.

"Good evening, Sir Guy," he said. "It is very near my moment, and you – Standy – all of you – have failed. Give me the syringe, if you please, Rosaine."

Standy held his breath. Sir Guy appeared to be quite indifferent, forcing himself to fix his gaze on one of the oak beams high up on the side of the farther wall of the room. And then, with a sense of suddenly slipping down into an abyss, they knew that they had failed. For Damian lifted the glass and flung the contents into Standy's face.

"You forgot that it was a new box of tablets, murderer!" he cried, triumphantly. "Some more hot water, Rosaine. Quickly – I have not much time."

They had failed. With a madman's cunning, Damian had counted the tablets in the box. Damian took the fresh glass of water from the girl, waited till the three tablets dissolved, filled the syringe, and plunged the needle deftly into his forearm. Then Damian went at once to the door. The time had passed for threats and triumphing. One thing alone possessed his mind – the end, now very near, of his gigantic task.

"I wish you goodbye, you fools," he said, very quietly. "I forgot the morphia, but I have forgotten nothing else. I would not advise you to follow me, gentlemen, for my entrances to the Pendine Caves are very dangerous places, and I know you will not dare to stop me. Those darling machines of mine are still running, still storing up their power for tomorrow, and only I, Carlo Damian, have the secret of their control. Only I, Carlo Damian, can stop them... Really, between ourselves, gentlemen," he finished with a savage and bitter irony, "I am by way of being an important man."

He was gone. They heard his footsteps outside, heard with an appalling sense of finality the opening of the wicket gate. Sir Guy turned to Standy with a shrug of his broad shoulders.

"You did your best, Standy," he said. "For a second I thought that you had saved us. I suppose," he added, "that is the last we shall see of Carlo Damian."

Suddenly the white face of Rosaine seemed the most vital thing in the room. She had risen. She was breathing a little heavily, and her beautiful hands were unsteady.

"I can help you!" she said. "Oh, thank Heaven, I believe I can help you! What he said made me remember. There is something else he has forgotten, and it's in the cottage still – I'm almost sure of it! There are other entrances to the Pendine Caves – a long way from those machines of his. He's forgotten the detailed plans of the caves he got when he bought the land years ago. They're here now, somewhere – I know I can find them!"

15

AT THE ELEVENTH HOUR

Windermaine hung in the outer realm of semiconsciousness for what seemed to him intolerable hours. He awoke to a world that was bounded by pain, barriered by harassing vacancies of thought. His brain was filled with a dull but omnipotent ache, as though a steel rivet was driven sheer through his head from temple to temple, and which every now and then fused into a red-hot heat.

He tried to sit up, and found, to his dumb surprise, that he was already sitting up. Damian had dumped him like that when he left him, a helpless heap of inanimate humanity, propped up against the rock wall on a flat bench. He tried to put his hands to his throbbing head. But he couldn't move his hands. They were secured fast to the steel legs of the bench, tied with twist after twist of wire.

The realisation brought him to with a jolt. The fog of torpor cleared from his brain, and he got something of a grip on his faculties. There was a lump the size of an egg at the back of his head, and his skull felt as though is was swelled up to bursting-point. He eased his head from its painful contact with the hard wall and forced himself to concentrate on his surroundings.

Across the end of the bench lay Damian's huge ulster. One side of it was turned back, revealing its heavy waterproof lining.

He raised his eyes from it and looked around. Damian himself was away at the far end, bending over the rotor of one of his machines, adjusting something in the bearings.

They were in the very centre of the great cave system, the long suspected but undiscovered section buried deep in the heart of the hill. Lights gleamed here and there from naked bulbs hanging on bare wires, stark streaks of lights that glared garishly in the blackness around. It was the largest cave in the entire system, a whole chain of caves linked into one. They opened out like a mammoth amphitheatre, and the only way in, or out, was through the down-flooding water of the fall.

All around rose the power-hum of the great generators, the ponderous, dynamo-like machines that created the fearful Disintegrator Force. It hummed in the air, low and sustained, but immensely dominant. The sound of the falls was almost eliminated. The acoustics of the place threw the sound back from the central cavern, but it still echoed faintly, like a distant chant through the long vaultings, even above the hum of the droning engines.

The generators were ranged in two long lines, connected with lengths of gleaming copper cables and linked up to a great battery of switch-boards on the walls. The giant accumulators, where all his vast reserves of the force were stored, were not visible. Either they were out of sight in the Stygian blackness overhead or in an adjoining cave. Gerry could not see them; he could only guess at their existence. And he took a crumb of consolation from the knowledge that if that force could actually be accumulated and stored away for later use there must at least be one alloy of metals against which the dreadful rays were powerless.

Damian was gone a long time. Windermaine could see him moving about among his humming machines like a great black bee in its hive, testing and screwing and adjusting wherever his skilled fingers touched. In the brighter glare of an arc lamp farther up, Gerry saw him more distinctly. He also saw something that explained the madman's immunity from Colt bullets. He was wearing a jerkin of mail. It covered his body from neck to knee, a casing of a treble thickness of chain links worn over a cuirass of hardened leather. The links overlapped in an intricate weave and they shone with a dull green glimmer under the hissing arc.

Windermaine waited in a cold perspiration. Whenever the madman looked across at him he feigned unconsciousness. Every minute he could hang fire down there was giving Standy a better chance of getting on his track – small enough hope though that was, so far as he was concerned.

Gerry was relying just then on his friend's undoubted flair for getting in ahead of the rest when everything pointed to his complete failure. There were instances in Standy's career when his quick ability to think out a situation and eliminate the false clues had amounted to genius. Twice he had saved Windermaine's life when the pair of them were out on the scent together. And, as events had developed in that last twenty-four hours of close-packed happenings, only Standy could save him again.

Damian came over at last and shook him.

"Wake! Wake up!" he said. "Time is slipping away and I have much to show you before you go back to the world of man beyond the moors. There is much that must be demonstrated and explained to you."

"Unfasten my hands," said Gerry, sullenly.

"No, no. You must stay there until you have seen the proofs I am about to show you. You are an unwilling witness; and I cannot attend to you and conduct my demonstrations too. You—"

"But I can't sit here listening to you while I'm trussed up like this," said Windermaine stormily. "I can't even see what you're doing. You've nearly screwed my head off against this filthy wall. Hang it all, I can't escape. You've got me down here and I can't get out. I can't dive through rock walls. Be sensible. Take these confounded wires off me and give me a chance to understand what you're talking about."

The madman seemed to ponder the matter for a moment. There was certainly something in the protest. But in the end he shook his head.

"No," he said, with polite finality. "I shall want you just where you are when I turn the rays on you. If you are moving about the radiations may damage my own machines. You will stay there. You can see the end of the bench without inconvenience. I will conduct my experiments there, under your eyes."

He dragged a test bench over from the other side and pushed it close to Gerry's feet. On the bench was a mass of paraphernalia, various metals in blocks, an assortment of stones and other materials. Clamped down at the end were two little machines no bigger than, as Damian had already declared, the magneto of a motor-car. They were made of a metal that was new to Windermaine. It seemed hard, iridescent, and it threw back the same greenish glimmer that came off his protective mail. Long wires reached away from behind them to an unseen point at the far end of the cave among the switch-boards.

"These," said the scientist, "are my toys, the tiny miniatures of the great machines you see all around you. They are the models on which the greater creations have been built. I use them for experiment only."

He spoke without bombast, without a spark of pride or vainglory. He was just a great scientist on a platform, delivering an unscientific lecture to a rather unintelligent audience.

He pointed to a four-inch ball of mercury that crowned each machine.

"The rays emanate from there," he explained. "The mercury is not contained in glass. It is free. The silver sphere you see there is a globe of mercury – solidified! For the purposes of these experiments I use both machines. One eliminates the force of cohesion: the other abolishes gravity. In the bigger machines over there the two principles are combined, producing the Disintegration Ray, the effect of which you have already seen in the Black Deep and elsewhere. The force is like electricity – it can travel along a wire. There is enough of it stored up in these caves to demolish an earth nearly twice the size of this. I will show you its effect on Harveyised gun steel."

He pushed a slab of steel to the end of the bench and propped it against the wall. The machine was nearly ten yards from it and there was no connecting wire. Damian adjusted a long funnel of the same dull green metal over the mercury ball, pointing to full at the slab of steel. He pushed over a switch in the base of the machine and instantly the mercury leapt into incandescent life. It flashed and scintillated with a bright emerald-green fire, exactly the same colour and brilliance that had puzzled the neighbourhood for weeks on the slopes of the Pendine Hills.

Windermaine watched with staring eyes. There was no sound, not even a hiss from the deadly thing. Only the vast, nerve-deadening humming of the mighty generators that loaded the air with the fearsome portent of their power – and the green, leaping iridescence flashing and streaming from the mouth of the funnel.

Windermaine looked, and looked again. The block of fiercely-hardened steel was slipping and creeping from its support against the wall – like ice melting before a furnace door. It was crumbling to powder before his eyes, falling to infinitesimal dust, to the very ashes of disintegration. In ten seconds it was gone; and then the end of the bench began to moulder too. Damian switched off the force.

"That was the effect you observed in the brown streak that ran across the moors" he continued. "The force was sent through an old Army field telegraph wire laid down during some manoeuvres a few months ago. Copper is the last metal to be affected. Nearly half an hour is required before copper begins to disintegrate.

"That fact alone makes possible the abolition of the earth. All over the world is a colossal system of wires. Telephones, telegraphs, electric light, tape machines, cables – the whole earth is a network of wires and rails. Into this amazing interlinkage of wiring I introduce the Disintegrator Force. And there is no insulation against it. Porcelain and rubber are conductors!

"In eight seconds the reservoirs of destruction penned up in these hills will be operating in every quarter of the earth. This force penetrates through a hundred feet of solid earth in a single second: that is, employing these little machines here. The penetrative force of the great power reserves, of course, I cannot compute. Roughly, I should imagine, about four thousand times the strength of the force you have already seen. Which means that in thirty-two seconds the entire world – mud, rivers, towns, mountains, people, everything in it and on it – will be reduced to the same indivisible dust you see there.

"The two great natural forces that hold the earth in being will have been destroyed. Cohesion, the force that held that steel block together, has been removed. The block crumbles to dust. Only the other great force, that of gravity, holds it on the earth at all. A thousandth of a second of the Degravitisor" – he touched the switch of the second machine – "and even the dust is gone!"

There was a sharp sound from the pile of dust, like the quick burst of magnesium powder in a flashlight, and the dust was blown high into the darkness overhead.

"And so will the world vanish," murmured the madman. "In a little while it will be nothing but a great ball of smashed atoms: a little while longer and even the atoms will be a vapour dispersed in its rush through unending space, a wisp of steam among the planets."

He threw other metals, other fabrics, in the orbit of the deadly rays. Windermaine watched them disintegrate. And then, all in a moment, he found himself frantically trying to take his eyes off the amazing things that were happening on that bench, trying to get his own eyes out of the range of Damian's vision. There was a wild surge of excitement plunging through him and he was terrified lest it showed in his eyes.

Unseen hands were at work under the bench quietly unfastening the wires that held him. He had seen no one, heard no one. So far as he knew he was alone in that vast amphitheatre of horrors, alone with a madman with every avenue of escape cut off. And yet without hint or warning someone had penetrated into those secret vaults, someone had beaten Damian at his own game, found the way through to his great sanctuary and was with him.

"Good old Standy!"

The thought thundered across his brain. Perspiration stood on his forehead. It was no hallucination, no trick of a brain tormented beyond its limits. He could feel the deft fingers working away at the wires, silent as a shadow. One hand was already free and skilled fingers were massaging the life back into his numbed veins.

"The wild swan got into the beam of the Anti-Cohesor," continued the demonstrator. "So did the hare. They were long-distance efforts, but entirely satisfactory – if unwitting. The sheep that vanished and perplexed the whole countryside were treated with the Degravitisor. The Black Deep was dried up with a mixture of both: the same mixture that will be used for the final demolition of the earth. If you will wait a moment I will bring a couple of live animals and you will see the effect of both rays on the living tissue. After that I will subject *you* to the rays and then you will learn for yourself."

He turned and walked sombrely away, on past the switchboards and out of the giant central cavern.

Windermaine felt his other hand slip free from its last gripping bond. He raised himself stiffly and peered over the edge of the bench. There was a face looking up at him, a face with red-rimmed eyes and a look of fear all over it.

"Good heavens – Rosaine!"

For a brief, wonder-filled moment Windermaine stared at the girl in a maze of hopeless incredulity.

Rosaine there, in that chamber of dread – Rosaine, apparently as much at home in the inner recesses of Damian's secret lair as she was in Rose Cottage. And, most devastating discovery of all – still with Carlo Damian.

Gerry broke into an incoherent string of babbled questionings, his brain grappling with the first phantoms of a wild surmise.

But Rosaine's finger was at her lips, and in her eyes a look of beseeching earnestness that was alive with its own warnings.

"Quiet! Quiet!" she muttered. "For Heaven's sake don't let Damian hear! If he finds me helping you, he will burn the very soul out of me."

"But – but—"

Windermaine's own voice had dropped to a breathless whisper.

"Don't stop to talk," she said. "There's little enough time as it is. Listen to me – and do all I tell you, or you will leave this place maimed for life. He's gone for some animals, hasn't he?"

She crawled out from under the bench.

"Yes – going to kill them for my benefit."

"Then he won't be back for about three minutes. He keeps his livestock in another cave at the end there, where it's warmer. You'd have time to get away now – but it wouldn't be much use. Either he would overtake you before you got out on to the moors again or, if you got away, he would turn the Disintegrator on you and annihilate you as you ran. No, you've got to fight him and beat him at his own game."

"Me?" said Gerry. "I couldn't fight that great mammoth. I'm not afraid to go in and have a mill with anyone – but Damian isn't natural. I emptied a whole bunch of bullets at him today and it seemed to do him good! No earthly use me fighting him – he could tie me up in knots."

"No, no. Not that kind of fighting. I know that's no good. I've seen him half-kill three ruffians who set on him one night as we were coming out here. You've got to use your brain. Your hands are free. Think out some way of catching him off his guard. You ought to be able to manage it. Don't let him even suspect it. The danger is dreadfully near now. I knew it was threatening – months ago. I've been linked up with this awful thing since before he came to Deepvale. I know what his plans are. I'm part of them. I'm talking with him almost every hour he lives. I know exactly what his motives and intentions are. And I've learned some things tonight that have frightened even me!"

"What things, Rosaine? Tell me – quickly!"

"This horrible scheme of his – this smashing up of the world – it is likely to happen at any minute."

"I know. He has already told me so. But he is going to mutilate *me* first and send me back to the world as a sort of living proof of what's going to happen to the rest of humanity before he pulls the switches over and obliterates the lot of them."

"Yes, I heard him. But he doesn't know what I know. His brain has become too warped to see the horrible danger that is rising up all around him. That awful cataclysm may strike the world at any moment – even now, while we're talking – it may happen *in spite of Carlo Damian* !"

"What? What on earth do you mean?"

"I mean that there are pressures mounting up in those accumulators that the accumulators themselves cannot stand. They are standing now at the bursting point. And he doesn't know it! He's too fanatically wrapped up in the larger issues even to glance at his gauges: I honestly believe he is so far gone that he doesn't recognise them, doesn't realise their significance. The whole thing is positively frightening. For three years now those accumulators have been charging. I was here when he built them: here when the generators first went into motion."

"Gerry!" – the word broke impulsively from her lips – "do you know what's happening out there in those storage caves? Those great accumulators are quivering, positively quivering with the fearful pressure of the power they contain. And I can't release it. All the forces of death and disruption are bottled up in those great batteries, and if they break through the world is doomed.

"Oh! the unspeakable years I've spent trying to prevent this – trying to hold it up. But in his madness, Gerry, he even turns on me. He watches me as a general watches a traitor. I can't move but his eyes are on me. There is nothing I can do."

The girl was almost distracted. She wrung her hands in an agony of helplessness.

"You mean that even if I killed the great brute here – now – tonight – nothing could stop the final catastrophe he has planned?" gasped Windermaine. He wras as much staggered as the girl by that new thunderbolt.

She looked round at the far end of the great cave.

"Yes!" she said, in a terrified whisper. "Unless these awful machines are stopped, before many hours have passed something awful will happen. The pressure-gauges are already jammed up tight. They must have been like it for days. And I can't even find out where he has tapped in on the outside wires. He's altered the entire plan of his switchboards since I was here last. The Madrid cable runs out across the Channel from Lynford. He has already made a connection into it, about a hundred yards out beyond the low-tide limit. I know that. He told me yesterday. But I can't find its contact on the switchboard. He has other lines out, too, but I know where they are. If that power bursts through, nothing on earth can save us."

Windermaine had taken her hands in his.

"Rosaine," he said, "I think there's a way out. And if there is – and I make it – I shall want to tell you what I think of you. May—"

"You – you won't *kill* him?" she interrupted.

"Perhaps – why? Would you be very grieved?"

She did not answer, but turned again and looked with fearful intensity towards the great cave entrance.

"Hush! Here he comes!" she gasped. "Careful now – sit as you were when he left you – hands down – bend them round the legs more. That's better. Head over on one side – strain your neck round – that's right – and for mercy's sake don't let him suspect you!"

She slid back under the bench.

By straining his neck round acutely he could just see the gaunt figure of Damian coming back into the main cavern. He appeared to be carrying two clumsy-looking boxes under his arms. In the nearer light only one was a box; the other was a kind of roughly-constructed wooden cage, about a yard square.

He put the box down on the floor and lifted the cage on to the bench. Inside was a little brown furry animal, growling and snapping at the bars in a shocking temper. The creature was either very frightened or amazingly courageous, for every now and then it set off on a wild whiz round the cage, flying from side to side with sudden jumps that shook the cage and almost defied the eye to follow.

"This," said Damian, placidly, "is a badger. A hardy little animal and one which, as you see, does not easily give up its independence. For some weeks I have been experimenting on live animals – to see if, by some extraordinary freak of nature, there should be one species that fails to succumb to the ray immediately. So far I have not found one that can withstand the Disintegrator for longer than one-tenth of a second – using nothing more than the miniatures I have already demonstrated."

"There's no need to kill that poor little creature," said Windermaine. "You've already shown me what your apparatus is capable of. I'm quite willing to believe the evidence of my own eyes. Why persist? Get to work on me and let me get out of this hole."

"But, my dear friend—"

"See here, Damian. You're only knocking at an open door. There's no point in bringing in dumb animals to slaughter in front of me; nothing fine or noble about it. The poor beast can't help itself. You're only re-proving a case you've already proved."

"What matter," said the madman, amiably, "if the badger dies now, or a few hours later, when all the rest of the animal kingdom perish? No. When I send you back to the world it is necessary that you should be able to tell them all. Without the proof of instant death on a living, virile animal, your testimony would be incomplete. In so great and so extraordinarily grave a matter as this it is best that every chance should be given to those about to die."

Windermaine sat back and said nothing. He was grinding his teeth at the wantonness of it. But his time had not come yet. A false move would have wrecked every hope. For the madman, though still his old unconcerned, studious self, was glancing around him in a nervous, apprehensive way.

It was as though the unbalanced brain had sensed a change in the atmosphere, a suble difference in Windermaine's bearing, and was looking for the cause of it. In losing so much, his brain had acquired something more, a highly-strung faculty of sensitiveness that played on him like wind on a violin string.

Windermaine was positive he suspected something. His attitude was tightening up every moment, and there was a lurking twist in his eyes that kept darting hither and thither while he prepared his experiments.

16

THE PITILESS RAY

Windermaine found himself wishing he had given Rosaine his revolver. Now that he had discovered the trick of the chain mail, it seemed to him that a bullet in Damian's brain would be the quickest way out of it. Pity he hadn't shot at his head before. And the way his eyes kept darting about, they were bound to alight before long on the girl under the bench.

"You must pardon the seeming delay," muttered Damian, almost to himself, "but I am anxious to demonstrate the powers of this ray at its fullest potency. For this experiment I am utilising both the Degravitisor and the Anti-Cohesor. Both forces are directed at the object simultaneously. The effect is exactly the same as that produced by the power output of the big machines. The cross contact is made between the two machines and the funnels are set – so! If you will wait till the animal is in a favourable attitude, I will demonstrate what happens when both rays are turned on him for a single second."

Windermaine could not help it. He was looking at the valiant little spitfire in spite of himself. It wasn't that he wanted to, but that he just couldn't take his eyes off the eerie things Damian was able to do with his ray.

The badger, unsettled by the glittering lights and the rumbling hum of the mighty machinery, had worked itself into a great state of excitement. It wasn't still for a moment, but, with its beady eyes flashing and its sharp-pointed teeth showing in a continual growl of sheer animal agression, it was bounding about the cage like a brown streak.

Damian waited for the little animal to come to a standstill. His finger was on the switch ready to press it the moment the fierce dance died down.

But the little fellow was giving no quarter. Its mad acrobatics didn't die down. Neither did they show any sign of doing so. On the contrary, it seemed as though the tough little beggar could keep it up all night.

Damian pressed the trigger, irritably.

Windermaine gasped. Badger, cage, and all vanished off the bench. That's all that could be said about it. They just vanished. There was no sound. The badger hadn't even time to voice its surprise or its pain. One moment it was on the bench; the next it was gone.

Gerry had been watching the whole thing intently. And he had taken particular note of what the badger was doing when the ray was switched on. The animal had just landed at the bottom of the cage in the far corner, and had turned. Just for a moment Windermaine had a close view of a clever, dapper little head crouching for a spring, and of a lithe, supple little body flexed for it. The badger sprang. And it was at that moment that Damian pressed the switch.

It was all over in a second. The current was on and off in a single flashing burst of green. But the badger never even reached the opposite bars. Its little body had been in actual flight when the switch went down. But it never reached the other side of the cage.

Gerry had been expecting the bump and the impact of the darting body on the wooden laths. But it never came. That badger leapt sheer out of life into oblivion. There was just the tiniest little swish of sound, as when a candle gutters out: it was not so much a sound in itself as a flicker of the silence.

Somewhere overhead, jammed hard against the roof, was a faint powdering of disintegration, attracted as firmly to the roof as previously it had been to the floor.

"You see?" said Damian. "Absolute and instantaneous annihilation. And I assure you there is no power known to science that can withstand its effect. That living organism was transmuted into weightless dust in the one-hundredth part of a second. That, I think, is a computation you might care to memorise for the benefit of those whose souls you have to save. Striking figures and arresting incidents count for much. The second animal experiment concerns a domestic pet. It is fair that you should see both types of animal under the ray."

He dumped the box heavily on the bench.

A querulous "Yap" came from inside the box. Windermaine felt the hair on the nape of his neck tingling. That doggy utterance sounded vaguely familiar to him.

"It is natural to suppose," went on Damian, "that a thoroughly domesticated animal like the dog, coming down to us through long generations of domesticated forbears, would not last as long under the ray as an animal in the wild state. But I maintain that complete disintegration occurs with such instantaneity that any comparison of time lapses is futile. You will see for yourself. This is quite an ordinary dog – a trifle snappy with strangers, perhaps, but that is a good fault in most Scottish breeds. This one was found wandering on the moors today."

Having cut away the cords, he knocked the lid off the box and hauled out a stumpy wire-haired terrier by the scruff of the neck. He was merry-eyed and cock-eared, with a fine straight chest-line and bandy legs in front. And he was white from whisker to tail-tip.

"Mack!" cried Windermaine from the end of the bench.

The little West Highlander waited for no more than that. This incontinent treatment of the last few hours was something altogether too disagreeable for words. He neither knew nor approved of the grim-visaged person who was responsible for it, but since dogs must always obey the human, he had put up with all sorts of highly unorthodox treatment.

With a high-pitched yelp of glad relief Mack made a jump to get across to his master. Damian, with a string round its neck, hauled him back. There was a snarl, a sudden flurry of white fur and compact flesh, and Damian was dancing round with a hand that was bitten through to the bone.

In a moment Mack was across on his master's chest, covering his face with a generous plastering of mad, glad, doggy kisses, whimpering his joy at the reunion, and with a tail that was nearly wagging itself off.

With a savage rumble in the chest Damian stamped across to recover the terrier. He leaned over Windermaine to take it again by the scruff of the neck – and Windermaine saw his chance.

The great throat was stretched out above him, and the man was more than half off his balance. With his hands outstretched to the dog, he was powerless and as "wide open" as a gate.

Windermaine swung a terrific blow at the centre of Damian's stretched throat. He whipped his hand away from the leg of the bench and swept it upwards with all his might, striking, not with the fist, but with the edge of his hand opened stiffly.

It is not a new trick. It is an old one; old as the hills; known in every port of the world from the Pool to the Behring Sea. But its effect is terrible. The point of aim is the Adam's apple. If it lands there truly and with sufficient force, death may easily supervene. The roots of the tongue are forced up into the mouth to such an extent that choking is practically inevitable.

Damian didn't choke. Windermaine, from his position, couldn't get sufficient force into the stroke for that. But it did quite well enough. The madman gasped and staggered back, one hand up-flung to his constricted throat. With his amazement at seeing his manacled prisoner suddenly free, and the shock of the impact on that bulging nerve centre, he went back, rocking on his heels.

And Windermaine was off the bench and after him at a bound. The only things he had to avoid were those enormous hands and arms. If they once got a hold on him there would be bones broken, and that would be the end of it so far as Gerry was concerned.

He swung a mighty right-handed blow to the jaw while his man was still off his balance. He was back again in the old days, with the gloves on, and a fellow as tough as himself in front of him, hot and eager for a two-fisted fight.

Damian pulled up short against the rock wall and Gerry slugged him again. Each hit was a palpable knock-out. Any ordinary man would have fallen like a sack of beans.

But for some inexplicable reason Damian was still on his feet, mystified, perhaps, at the astonishing weight of punching power carried in the younger man's shoulders, but still – on his feet.

Gerry was seeing through a red mist, a sea of red that swept in and submerged him. He jumped in through the cumbersomely swinging arms, and got at the madman's throat. As well strangle the brute, he argued, as knock him out. There was no room on the earth for such a ghoul as Damian – not with Rosaine still there, under the bench...

Damian began kicking, lunging out ferociously with his steel-shod boots. Gerry was hopping about like a dancing Dervish trying to avoid them. There would be smashed bones wherever those fierce boots connected. But it was impossible for him to dodge those flailing feet and hang on to the straining throat too. Something had to be done.

"Mack! At him!" he yelled. "Into him!"

The terrier streaked into the fray like a white-hot arrow. Straight at the flying feet he went, and thereafter Damian's legs were too busy seeking their own salvation to give Windermaine any further trouble.

Then, from under the bench, like a revolver crack in a silent room, came a warning shout, urgent, electrically imperative.

"Gerry! Look out! The spanner!"

Windermaine jarred his head to one side as the spanner fell, crunching into his shoulder. The red mist cleared for a brief moment and then overwhelmed him again. With an angry growl he lunged upwards again at the massive jaw. The blow went home with a staccato smack. Damian's eyes glazed and he tottered over in a sprawling heap.

Windermaine whipped out his gun as he fell, and rammed it against the madman's forehead. The red mist glowed hot. It was burning him, scorching into him the desire to kill.

There was a scurry across the floor and an agonized panting past his ear. The gun was twisted out of his flexing hand.

"Not – not that!" gasped Rosaine. "Not killing – no – oh, please, not that!"

"Why not?" demanded Windermaine savagely, wheeling on her as though he would have smashed her too. "Why not? Eh? Answer me? What is this great devil to you?"

Only faintly he caught the whisper as she fell reeling to the floor.

"He – is – my father!"

17

LOVE CONFESSED

Windermaine reeled back and stared down at the pathetic little heap of femininity at his feet.

Her words had come to him in a half-frightened whisper, barely audible above the roar of the generators: but they had shouted their way across his brain peals of thunder.

They set every fibre within him tingling and ringing to an exultant note.

To her it was a confession, torn from unwilling lips: to him it was a song-burst, a triumphant paean that echoed again and again through the secret chambers of his soul.

The red mist was fading from his burning eyes; the lusting madness for slaughter was lifting from him like a dawn haze at sea when the sun breaks through.

It was as though a great light of understanding had burnt through to his inner self, stemming his savagery, putting a sudden leash upon his wrath.

In that blazing second he saw the whole pitiful story that lay behind her silence, the tender, pathetic strength of the loyalty that bound her.

Daughter of the most appalling imbecile the world has ever known! That was the full context of it, crystallised and hardened into a single sentence.

He saw the full horror and the agony the years had thrust upon her. The finger of accusing scorn pointing for ever, mercilessly, at the insanity taint. "Her father was a lunatic." He could hear the poison tongues saying it with relish, saying it as they had already said, "She is living with a man."

And what a lunatic! A man with the brain of a monster. A man who had terrorised a countryside, who had broken the killing law, and, who, throughout every day of a long decade, had bent his marvellous powers to the annihilation of common humanity.

It had cost her good name, lost it irrevocably to the world outside: robbed her of every shining hope and ambition that reigns in the heart of woman. Love, home, hope, happiness – they were golden crowns unknown to her. Her whole life was dedicated to the service of a madman. He could just begin to realise the awful burden she had borne, without murmuring, through the sweet years of her life.

The slow realisation of the knowledge that her father was gone beyond all hope; the horrified understanding of the tendency his insanity was taking; the ghastly fear of the hand of the law reaching out for him relentlessly, inexorably; her unending struggles to coax his reason back and hide it from the rest of the world; her ceaseless efforts to wean his mind from the fearful undertaking he had embarked upon; the tortuous subterfuges to get him away into the country – and then the final horror when realisation came to her that even out there, in one of the wildest places of the moors, she had found for him the perfect retreat for the furtherance of his plans – the world's perfect workshop. A focusing point for all he hoped to do and conceive – where even the thunder of the falls killed off the tell-tale rumble of his droning engines.

He was trembling badly as he stooped and picked her up, a frail little armful of tenderness, whose only sin was that she had loved too well.

He laid her on the bench and stood by her, amid the throb and roar of the mighty machines that were forcing up the powers of death all around them, the drone of the spinning rotors, the thrust and return of oiled connecting rods, the high whinny of copper drums speeding round at a pace so terrific that they appeared to be slowly revolving the other way, the sharp hiss of compressed air spitting from the safety valves – and the soft organ note of the distant falling water over all.

When she came to she was lying in his arms. His face was above her and his eyes were full of the wonder stories the world had denied her so long. He was telling them to her, silently, with no more than the tensity of his look and the reverence in his eyes. Her eyelids closed, and she lay back, breathing softly. It was woman's inimitable gesture of willing, exquisite surrender.

He began talking to her, quickly, eagerly, putting the stories into his own unhesitant words, painting thought-pictures for her in a world that was one great garden, rose-clustered, lily-fair, filled with the perfumes of Araby.

Unmindful of the straining pressure-gauges, heedless of the cataclysm that was on the point of bursting in flame and heat all around them, they trod the shining highways that are known only to those who have come through the gates of Arcady.

And when he finally stopped, her eyes were very bright, and glistening with the tears that come when enchantment has thralled the soul beyond restraint. She pushed him away, gently, the pressure of a burning kiss still on her lips, lingering there like the impress of a warm rose.

He stood up and held out his hands to her, helping her to rise. And in his mind there was not one single thought for Valerie: he did not even .remember the existence of the girl who had promised herself to him, in the presence of a father who was already standing in the shadows of the forecourt of death.

He had not even a thought to spare for the giant figure of the madman who, just behind him, was fast stirring into consciousness.

"Till tomorrow?" he whispered.

And she nodded, half-shyly.

"Where?" he said, with a twinkle beginning to come into his eyes. "By the wicket gate?"

She reddened and then smiled back at him.

"At four o'clock," she said. "I shall be there this time, Gerry."

He wrapped the great ulster round her and led her back towards the waterfall.

"There is a lot to be done here yet, dear," he said, gently. "A lot of unpleasant things, and – well, I don't want you to be here."

"I'm not afraid of danger, Gerry," she said, quietly. "Half my life seems to have been spent playing with death."

"Not that, little one," he replied. "It's Standy. I'll have to get him here – and I don't want you here when he comes. You are out of this, so far as the law is concerned. And it's man's work, anyhow. Wish to goodness I knew how to stop those infernal machines."

"There is no way!" said Rosaine. "There is a dynamo action in them. They make their own electricity – they create their own driving power while they are going. They never have been stopped. They will run and run and run until they just run themselves to a standstill. I've heard him say so, proudly, heaps of times."

"And you've no idea how that ray can be cut off from the machines making it?"

"I'm afraid there's no way to do that either. The machines are all coupled direct to the accumulators."

"Then we shall have to find a way," he said flatly. "This horror has got to be ended tonight or—"

"Or what, Gerry?"

"Or there will be no four o'clock tomorrow, little woman, nor even a wicket gate for you and me to keep our tryst beside."

They had reached the falling curtain of water. He kissed her once, twice, passionately.

"Goodnight, my dearest," he said.

"Till tomorrow," she whispered back. She squeezed his hand in the darkness: and he was alone.

He hurried back to the great central cave. From some distance away he heard Mack barking, a sharp staccato yelp of alarm. He ran. The madman was on his knees, staggering shakily to his feet.

Windermaine was on top of him like a scrum half. Damian was still dizzy or Gerry could never have done what he did. He gave him a taste of his own medicine. In five frantic minutes he had been pinioned with his own wires. His hands were bound behind him, and his feet, from knees to ankles, were wrapped round and round in an inextricable mass of it.

Gerry sat back on the bench and regarded his handiwork.

"Not bad for a landsman," he commented. "Used rather more material than Standy would have done, but the effect is achieved. Mr. Damian, if you will do me the favour of giving me your full and unstinted attention for a few moments, I'd be obliged. There are a few questions I have to ask you – and I must request you to give me your answers as quickly as may be possible, in strict conformity with the higher tenets of truth. To begin with, how do you stop these pestiferous machines of yours from churning out their beastly rays?"

Damian eyed him with sullen animosity. Flat on his back and unable to move a limb, he just lay and glared his hatred at the man who had broken through his guard, the man who was within an ace of beating him on the post. And the hate in his eyes was animal. He was straining at his bonds like a netted python.

Windermaine repeated his question stolidly. A gleam of malignant triumph shone on the madman's face.

"So," he rumbled, throatily, "you are frightened? The fear of death is upon you? And well it might be!"

He broke into loud peals of dreadful laughter.

"You are too late!" he croaked. "Nothing can save you now. There is no hope for you. The sands are running out. There are but a few minutes between you and all eternity!"

"How do you stop that?" repeated Gerry.

"Fool – shall I tell *you*? You who would not carry the news? You – the last Judas of all?"

Windermaine's hand had gone out to the machine on the bench. It was the awful De-coheser.

"You fixed it like this, didn't you" he said, placidly. He screwed it round on its clamps and adjusted the funnel so that it pointed full at the madman's writhing body. Then he turned it till its outer edge was just clear of his feet. He looked down at Damian.

A swift and tremendous change had come over the man. A livid, ghastly whiteness had swept over him. His face was bloodless with a gripping fear. Even the sallow saturninity was gone. There was nothing left but the skintight mask of fear that had smothered the triumph out of him.

"A quick-change artiste, too, I see," observed Gerry.

He pushed the switch over. The shimmering green radiance leapt to life in the funnel mouth, quivering there like a piece of green rainbow. It centred on a little patch on the floor, a few inches beyond the madman's toes. The granite crumbled to dust under the rays – the little patch *simmered* under Windermaine's eyes.

He moved the beam along till it just touched the heel of Damian's shoe. The heel vanished.

The madman screamed curses at the man above him.

"And lacks humour," murmured the younger man. "I'd have thought you'd have been the first to appreciate a quick trip to eternity. You're keen enough to sent others there. Come on, now – before you lose your feet! How do you stop them?"

He turned the beam the shade of an inch.

And the soles powdered softly off the great boots.

"Quickly, Damian," he said. "It will be your ankles next."

The madman broke down.

"The machine!" he shrieked. "The machine! There is no other way!"

"You swear on that?"

"Yes – yes. I swear – there is nothing else that can stop them."

"Which machine?" queried Gerry, in a flat, calm voice.

"Oh, forgive me!" Damian was sobbing in his impotent helplessness. "The one in your hands!"

Gerry relaxed.

"Fancy not thinking of that before," he said, deprecatingly. "So jolly simple, too."

18

DAMIAN'S LAST THROW

Outside, under the vast tiering of the Pendine Caves, Standy waited on in the darkness.

The minutes had dragged interminably since he had taken up his vigil there. He was waiting for just one thing. When that happened he was going in through that great downflood of water, whether his forces had arrived or not.

One by one dim figures began to drift through the darkness. They were hurrying silently, coming in from all directions. Standy brought them over to the entrance cave with a quick flash of his torch. First came the sergeant from Bannicombe village, sceptical to the point of sarcastic unbelief. Not that he couldn't believe facts. He could – provided he read them in his Sunday paper as happening a hundred miles away. Gigantic interludes did not squeeze themselves into *his* orbit. He wasn't important enough. The whole thing was a hoax.

A straggle of civilians came next, more curious than partisan. They had heard about it down in the hamlets and didn't want to be out of any fun that was going on.

The news that a great Scotland Yard detective was up there waiting for them at the Pendines cleared the local taprooms as by magic. Then a couple of constables, plodding solidly through the gorse. And then the main detachment from

Lynford. Standy made them get well under cover of the great boulders that strewed the entrances.

Last of all came Tendleton, a couple of pounds lighter already, and breathing stertorously.

"Get through to London?" whispered Standy.

"Yes, sir. Told Mr. Drake all you said."

"Good. He's sending immediately?"

"Said he'd have two car loads on the road before I was out of the box!" said the constable, aggrievedly.

"Reckon they'll be too late after all," commented Standy. "Except to help us mop up the débris."

"Are you going in, sir?" asked the unbeliever.

"Not yet. I'll tell you when – after—"

Hurrying footsteps sounded from the darkness of the cave interior. Heads crouched lower behind the rocks. Here and there a face peeped out, scared, but determined to miss nothing.

A little figure appeared, dainty and trim even in the folds of the drenched ulster. Her hair was wet and her shoes squelched water. She glanced round hurriedly to see that the way was clear and then stepped out quickly in the direction of Rose Cottage.

Tendleton reared up ponderously. There was something *he* could tackle, something considerably nearer his mark than the sinister possibilities of the mad scientist.

"That's his gal," he announced. "I'll get her, anyway."

Standy pulled him back viciously.

"Down, you fat fool! That girl is all I've been waiting for. She's come out! Don't you see what that means? It means that Windermaine is getting away with it. He's safe – or she'd never have left the caves. She's marvellously in love with Windermaine. She'd have stayed in there and died sooner than have left *him*! Windermaine's top dog – he's doing the big smash on his own. He'd have bashed the life out of me if I'd let the girl be dragged into this business. There'll be inquests and

Heaven knows what not. Come oh, boys, she's clear by now. In with you! Follow my torch, and, when you come to the falls, jump!"

Candles and storm lamps were lit, throwing pools of light and long darting shadows like leaping rods of jet among the granite buttresses. The party moved off, Standy ahead and Tendleton immediately behind the last but one.

Once they lost their way completely and had to go back almost to the entrance before they picked up the right trail again. And once again one of the volunteers slipped on a jutment of loose rubble and cracked a bone in his leg. Two others waited behind with him, for none of them cared about facing the Pendine horror alone. The mishaps occasioned delays, and it was nearly an hour before the lights were shining on the sheeting blackness of the falls.

Some of the volunteers didn't seem to be exactly thrilled with the idea of making that blind plunge through the crashing water. It seemed like taking a cold, suicidal step right off the edge of the earth and into the eternity of spaceless night beyond.

But Standy wasn't waiting. Others had done it – and they they were all human. He drew in a deep breath, jammed his bowler hard down on his head, and jumped. He landed on the other side on his knees, breathless and gasping. The water was like liquid ice. To his amazement the next one to crash through was Tendleton.

Standy laughed right down in his chest and grabbed him by the arm.

"Come on, old war horse," he said. "You're my meat."

Tendlcton was game. He had made the plunge and the bit was between his teeth. This was great stuff! This was fame! He would be in the headlines in the morning. Standy was the man to stand by, anyway. He knew what he was up to. He wasn't running his head into any more trouble than he could comfortably handle. And Tendleton was with him – up to the neck.

Together they ran through the great rock corridors and burst into the lighted amphitheatre. They stood still in utter amazement, a little trickle of water running coldly down Standy's neck from the uptilted curve of his bowler.

Damian, trussed up like a fowl, was lying full length on the floor, shrieking, sobbing, screaming in a transport of demoniacal frenzy. His wrists were cut to the bone by the wires; his eyes were rolling wildly. And all around him was a scene of fearful destruction.

In the air hung a thick, swirling fog of brassy dust, through which the lamps shone with a dull, unearthly glow, like pools of dim gold in a vault of coppery gloom. The hum of the giant rotors was dying out. Fresh banks of the seething fog broke out in rolling clouds from the far end. They coincided with muffled explosions that seemed to drift to the ear through immense blanketing folds of silence.

Through the swirling mist wraiths they caught fleeting glimpses of a tall, dishevelled figure diving in and out of the fog, with a little black machine in his hands and a wire that trailed away behind him. His face was glistening with perspiration, for the heat generated by the suddenly atomized metals was terrific. The brassy dust was caked thick on his face and matted into his hair; he gleamed like a brazen statue in the sheen of light.

In and out of the lines of racing machines he plunged while new clouds of choking dust and new drum-like explosions marked his passage. Through the flying particles a faint green flicker shone, bobbing up every now and then like a will o' the wisp in the gloom.

Suddenly, with a final effort of demented strength, a herculean spasm of mighty muscle power that shook him like a reed, the madman burst the wires that bound his hands.

Slavering at the mouth, he began clawing his way along the floor, his maddened eyes fixed in a red glare on the other machine on the bench. The humming was dying out to a faint, trembling tremor in the air. Windermaine couldn't see him. He was lost in the brazen clouds of the bursting machines.

"For Heaven's sake!" gasped Tendleton.

The words seemed to galvanise Standy into action. For a few moments he had been standing there, stupefied, unable to move, with his fingers still gripping hard on the constable's arm. But the human voice jarred him back. He plunged forward through the fog.

"Gerry!" he yelled. "Quick! He's got loose!"

He fell on the maniac and closed with him. But the superhuman strength of the insane was in Damian's bones. He flung Standy aside like a rat. His great fingers clutched up at the Degravitisor and wrenched it from the clamps.

He turned it full and square in the direction of Windermaine. He got the switch over – but nothing happened. For both Tendleton and Standy in a burst of mutual inspiration had seized at the feed wire and flung themselves forward, smashing it from its connections.

A few seconds later the reinforcements arrived, and Damian was secured. He died almost before the third pair of handcuffs were snapped on. His last tremendous frenzy had burst a blood-vessel.

The last humming note died into silence. The last terrible machine was pulverised, disintegrated back into its original electrons. The Horror of the Moors was dissipated for ever.

Windermaine emerged through the whirling dust, mopping his streaming face, astonished to see the crowd.

"O.K., laddie?" asked Standy.

"Phew! Yes. When did you get here?"

"Soon after the little visitor got clear."

Windermaine looked at him hard.

"Good old Standy," he muttered.

"Better go back and see her, hadn't you?"

Windermaine thrust the De-cohesor in his hands.

"You work it with that switch," he said. "There's a half-mile of accumulators, nearly bursting with death, in that outer cave through there," he said. "You may blow yourself and all creation to blazes – but the world won't be safe till they're smashed. Good luck, old scout. I'll see you later."

"But not at the wicket gate, I'll lay," grunted Standy.

He took the machine, eyeing it askance.

"Hey! Gerry!" he called.

But Windermaine was gone.

A soft light was burning in the window of Rose Cottage when Windermaine reached it. He knocked, and Rosaine came out to him.

Very gently he told her of the things that had happened in the Pendine Caves. He told her of the break-up of the great machines, of the coming demolition of the mighty accumulators – and then more gently still of the broken, dead thing they had left on the rock floor by the bench.

She did not weep. She was past all tears of sorrow. After all, it was the only way out, a solution that was as inevitable as the push and pull of the planets.

"It simply means this, little sweetheart," Gerry said. "You will be here tomorrow at four o'clock by the wicket gate, just as we arranged – *but* – you will never go back into Rose Cottage again. You will have all your trunks and things packed. And I shall be here with a car. There will be inquests – police inquiries – you understand, little lassie? Standy has been wonderful – to both of us. He has managed it – I got the broadest hint tonight. You don't even come into it at all. But you must not stay here. You must go away."

"With you, Gerry?"

"Yes, dearest, tomorrow. Standy is up there now—"

He broke off as a thunder of echoes roared to life along the crest of the Pendine Hills. There was a great green flash, brilliant, eye-aching, terrific – as though a vortex had opened in the soul of the hills and a great spouting volcano had burst into green, pulsing fire. They stood gazing at its awesome splendour.

And then it was gone.

"That's Standy's last word in the matter," said Gerry, quietly.

It was Gerry heard all about it next morning; how the volunteers had taken the great containers from the caves, out through the fall and up to the crest of the hill, and how, having stacked them up in a great quivering line, Standy had turned both rays on them at once, a force that annihilated even the forces of annihilation.

Valerie came in to him. Wagging tongues had spread the story through the village. She had seen, too, the flash on the hills and she came to him, half-nervously, with questions on her lips and in her eyes.

Windermaine remembered her with a shock. Almost before he knew it he was badly out of his depth, floundering about in a sea of embarrassments. He heard himself muttering broken, disjointed things, silly, inane things about promises of marriage, impossible situations, utmost discretions, difficulties that were fully understood, and assurances of his utter disavowal of the whole thing.

And through it all it began to dawn on him that Valerie was smiling at him shyly, uncomfortably, with lips that were self-conscious and eyes that were very bright. She was looking down at her left hand. The fingers of her right were twiddling a neat little band of plain platinum on the third finger.

Gerry did not remember much of what happened after that. He was travelling through a world that had suddenly gone a trifle hazy. He knew that he talked to her for a long time, with a chant of delirious relief ringing through his brain. And that afterwards Standy came in with a crowd of special correspondents at his heels, and that he talked to them all for what seemed hours.

The only thing he did remember definitely was when he stepped out of the car at the wicket gate. But that is a memory that concerns him alone – and one other: the girl who, more like a dainty little fragment of Dresden china than ever, was peeping mischievously over the gate at him.

A fan of Sherlock Holmes?
Then meet Solar Pons

The original fan fiction from the great August Derleth—the Sherlock Holmes of Praed Street.

“the best substitutes for Sherlock Holmes known.”
– Vincent Starrett

“an excellent series of adventures in detection in their own right.” – *The Chicago Tribune*

For more details and a full list of titles:
visit https://www.hachetteindia.com/home/yellowbacks